Fog Island Mountains

FOG ISLAND
MOUNTAINS

a novel

BY

M<small>ICHELLE</small> B<small>AILAT</small>-J<small>ONES</small>

Tantor
m e d i a

for Claude & Emiline

This is a work of fiction. All characters, organizations, and events portrayed in this
novel are either products of the author's imagination or used fictitiously.

Tantor Media, Inc.
6 Business Park Road
Old Saybrook, CT 06475

tantor.com
tantorpublishing.com

Fog Island Mountains

Copyright © 2014 by Michelle Bailat-Jones

Author photo © Danielle Libine

Design by Amy Fernald

ISBN: 9781630150020

Printed in the United States of America

First Tantor Media Printing, November 2014

Contents

霧島Kirishima

"A land where the morning sun shines directly, a land where the rays of the evening sun are brilliant. This is a most excellent place."

—Kojiki, Japan's "Record of Ancient Matters"

霧島Kirishima

A small chain of volcanic mountains that dot the southern half of Japan's island of Kyūshū. The chain is named after its second-highest peak, Mt. Kirishima.

霧島Kirishima

The Fog Island Mountains

Disturbed Weather

So this is our town, our little Komachi, this little cluster of businesses and houses settled into streets carved out of this volcanic soil, and crisscrossing each other, as we do, as our lives intersect from business to house to supermarket to hospital. And here, today, the wind has already begun to blow, a warning of the approaching typhoon. We are used to these storms, even if they have predicted this one will be big. They say this often, and often they are wrong, although I prefer to be careful, I will tape my windows and buy extra batteries for my flashlights. Because when they do hit, when they strike down on our clumsy structures and on our inept and inelegant lives, these winds do not show much mercy.

Until this great wind comes, the weather will be unstable, as we always are, not needing the excuse of pressure changes or ocean currents. We will watch the sticky, drizzly rain, the green clouds and gusts of wind that hit hard but do not build, not yet, these pre-winds will blow through town and leave us all hanging, waiting, leave us in an uncomfortable stillness, a trapped moment of *matte imasu*. Yes, waiting. This waiting the hardest part, and here is Alec Chester, one half of the subject of my poem, of this story that I must tell—don't worry about me yet, we will get to me soon—and he is watching through a window, watching out to avoid looking in, watching to calm his waiting.

There out the window, a girl, a little one, and he is watching her walk from a car at the edge of the parking lot, crossing over toward this building where he sits in a room—yes, still waiting. And she is coming to the hospital entrance below him, struggling against the rising wind, holding down the unruly panels of her school uniform skirt as it twists and puffs, disobeys, here a flash of cotton panties, the pale sticks of her legs. Her other hand is gripped tight to her father's but the man doesn't notice her struggle and Alec wants to knock against the glass of this examination room window, wants to slide open the locked panels and stick his head out into the sky and cup his hands around his mouth to shout, Hey, over there! Yes, you! Help her, she's yours to take care of.

"This is difficult, Alec." So says Shingo Ishikawa, a doctor in our mountain town.

"Just tell me." Alec's glance now pulled from the window, now back in the room, his time for waiting over.

Ishikawa is closing a file folder, sealing Alec's illness between the pressed stock of its hard yellow pulp, and all Alec can do is look at the man's ragged fingernails, at the red inflamed skin of this doctor's nail beds—how has he never noticed this nervous habit, in all the years of their friendship in this small town—but Ishikawa is stalling, is trying for more time. He'd hoped to wait for Kanae, he says, he wants to discuss this news with both of them because, and this he does not say out loud, a couple should face these words together. This is what he thinks, and what Alec feels, too, but Alec can only frown and say that she was supposed to meet him here, in this room. She was supposed to do this waiting with him, and he wonders if her presence here could prevent what is about to come.

"I don't know where she is, maybe she forgot." This said in frustration.
A too-quick response from Ishikawa. "She is nervous, women are fragile."

Oh, what a statement, made worse as neither man believes it, this predictable phrase meant to comfort men with diseases and injuries, a way to trick them into thinking they are still in control, and Alec nods, only because he doesn't want to argue with his friend, this man to whom he has taught English over the years in our small town. A friendship based on the translation of thought and idea back and forth and forth and back again, Japanese to English, English to Japanese, meaning faithfully replicated with a new sound, meaning sometimes, often, inevitably shifted. This is their friendship, a friendship based on rewording every phrase each man has ever said. But he knows, yes, our Alec knows, that Kanae is not fragile, compared to most, but especially compared to him, she has always been the stronger of the two.

"Okay," says Alec. "Okay." Again and again, he says this word *okay*. Then a pause. A glance. A twist of hands. Those ragged nail beds. Then, "Just tell me. Tell me. I know it's not good news."

So Ishikawa has no choice but to nod and pronounce a single word, a word that Alec knew he would hear but hoped he would not, and Ishikawa does not say the word again because once is always enough, and instead he begins to gesture, he circles up and around, cutting through the air of this doctor's office, over his own body with those angry hangnails and delicate fingers, and he is saying that it has spread already, that it has moved to other places in Alec's body. He is saying they believe it is everywhere.

Now we are watching Alec carefully, because his face is blank but his body has understood, and this is so curious, so horrific and sublime, that we can't help but look for his shoulders to tighten, his elbows to press against his sides and his hands to come together against his belly into little claws. Hands that want to conceal the original birthplace of this cancer's everywhere, wanting to cover it and hush it, to batten down the hatches because isn't this what a person does when a storm is about to hit? Don't we seal ourselves up and keep an eye out for leaks?

"I do not want to say anything else until we have more information." This Ishikawa is a humanist of the most brutal variety. "I don't want to give you false hope."

Alec, still flexing his claws, is looking at the white buttons of Ishikawa's lab coat, what courage, he is thinking, to give this information without breaking eye contact, because he—Alec—could never do this, could never be so categorical; he is thinking of his students, of his own stock phrases of "study harder" and "you'll get it, just spend more time." And he wonders then why he hasn't told Mrs. Nishikokubaru, his worst student, an absolute failure at forming English words and sentences, why hasn't he told her to give up, to get out, the whole thing is pointless, stop wasting my time, find a new hobby. Could he do this?

Over to the door, where Ishikawa turns and says in English, a testament to their friendship, "I am . . . I am so sorry, Alec."

What a thing to say but Alec is nodding, yes, thank you, yes, but ashamed now, burning with shame and looking at the floor because he has never managed to help Ishikawa lose that dreadful accent.

Alone now, Alec is back to checking the window, the little girl nowhere to be seen and presumably the hospital has taken her up into its maze of healing, and so he lets out a little breath, unclenches those belly-covering claws, closes his eyes and knows that she will be safe, she will be fine. Now he opens his eyes and must reach for one of his own children, his favorite—*shhh*, no parent has a favorite—but wait, first quickly again Kanae, his absent wife, dialing her number, listening to the ring, no answer, where could she be, why is she late? So now Megumi, his oldest, and while the telephone beeps and hums in his ear he is wondering again about that word "everywhere" and whether he will be able to pronounce it, whether he will be able to let it inside his mouth and form upon his tongue.

"Dad, I'm running out the door. I've got five minutes."

Such joy at the sound of her voice, this is his Meg, his artist-and-a-teacher-on-the-side, whose work is becoming famous on our island, her paintings with their uneasy colors and burnished silver backgrounds, her thickly painted-over fabrics and those hints of volcanic ridges and gauzy steam. He asks her about her mother, has she seen her, did they have plans? Tomorrow, Meg says, impatient—his Meg is almost always impatient, how has this happened, she was the happiest, the most exuberant of children—she needs to know if Kanae is coming to see her tomorrow.

"Is she coming to Jun's Kendo match or not?" This said nearly in anger.
"If she said she would come, she'll come."

Alec's fingers on the phone have gone tight not just at this questioning of Kanae's promise but at the mention of his grandchild, he pulls at them with his other hand, he relaxes them with effort and pictures his Jun, this bastard child, an unnamed little man with a round belly and those chestnut eyes, this happy toddler from an unknown union, a secret his daughter is keeping from them all. It hurts, even today, even with this everywhere scraping at his vocal chords, Alec is thinking he has a right to know who Jun is, and a right to know something of the man Megumi allowed inside her body, allowed to create life in her and bring that life into their family, but these are words that cannot be spoken, words as dangerous as Dr. Ishikawa's "everywhere" and "false hope."

So they are passing promises back and forth for a future visit, they are saying good-bye for now, both silenced with their harbored secrets and Alec now panicking to leave this room, to exit our rural hospital, to get himself out into the wind and the gathering clouds, to find his Kanae. Seconds later he is standing at the nursing station, making his appointment with Nurse Uchida who is also one of his students, as so many of us are in Komachi, and she will be kind to him, I think, I hope—and, yes, alas, Alec is going to need her kindness.

霧島

But here she is on a mountain road, Kanae Chester, we know exactly where to find her as Alec's appointment is about to start because she is a woman who keeps her promises, she is a woman driving down a badly tarmacked road and ready to join her husband at the hospital. Her body still overheated from the thermal baths at Kurokawa, her ears still ringing with the laughter of her friends, these women who join her each Thursday for a soak in the volcanic waters, her face now tired out and sagging from the work of forming itself into a mask that would hide her worry from her old friends. She is pulling into the parking lot and she sees that little girl mistreated by the gathering winds and she wonders what this young girl's father could be thinking about that he doesn't notice his daughter's one-armed resistance, but Kanae doesn't see Alec at the window and he does not see her, and it doesn't matter because she is already turning her car around and driving back up the same slick gray road, back up to Kurokawa Onsen and back into the hot water that numbs as it burns.

Kanae's turn to stare out a window—counting the tips of the pine trees along the ridge of the mountain and thinking how lovely is this place, how lucky she has been to live her life amidst such beauty, and to have been such a beauty; she is not thinking this last thought but it is a secret part of her, one of the reasons for the long straight line of her sixty-four years of happiness.

Alec is sixty-seven years old.
Alec is sick.
Alec is going to leave her behind.

Quickly out of the water again and back into her car, heading off this time to fix her broken promise but she doesn't get far, she is just as soon pulling the car into a viewpoint and then dialing, then listening, and then she is snapping shut the little clamshell of her cell phone, she is thinking, now I am sure, because this is why she has called him, this is why she's listened to his voice, his voice after his appointment, this is why she hasn't said a word, because his hello was enough, because now she is sure, and now she is nudging the car back out onto the road, repositioning the car in her own lane and ignoring an angry honk from an oncoming driver. What matters is the speed of her car and its position in the lane, what matters is the beat of the wipers and the hiss of hot wind against her car doors, what matters is driving carefully down a mountain road.

Kanae turns the radio on, she turns it off, she checks her rearview mirror, and with a breath she leans into the steering wheel, bearing down on the accelerator, faster and faster, following this road away from Kurokawa, driving blind, driving with only one thought—where can she stop—because hers is a jerky anxious flight, a flight of pauses and indecision. And here it is, this small noodle shop on the backside of the mountain, a cabin for tourists when the season is right, but thankfully empty tonight, when the season is wrong. Kanae pushes against the glass door and the bells jingle above her head and the owner is shouting *irasshaimase!* and the smells of the oil and the broth and the wheat of the noodles bear down on her and she is ashamed to feel so relieved.

Another window to distract her beside the table she has selected, and outside the starlings are gathering into a cloud against the purple sky, and they swoop and vibrate in the hot air. There are two birds out of sync with the undulating mass, and she watches, curious, as the birds fly in figures, in funnels and pressed circles, in shapes with blurred edges. She cannot think of the last time she sat in a restaurant by herself, and this thought leads to another so she wonders what else, what other phenomena has she missed by always having someone to keep her company, and now, here it is, Kanae's intuition expressed in the movement of her hand to her cheek, in the unsteady brush of a finger toward her ear—she has understood, she quickly closes her eyes.

Out of the darkness she hears, "Endo-san?"

She is turning, opening her eyes, no one has called her this in nearly forty years, not since her wedding, not since the perfect transformation she achieved when she agreed to exchange her family name for the foreign-sounding name of Chester, and so she blinks, she doesn't recognize the man standing at her table. He can tell.

"Your old neighbor, it's me . . . Fumi."

Oh yes, Fumikaze, she says, she can see him now, those watery eyes, the long bone of his nose, she is smiling—how is she smiling—but he smiles back at her, is reaching for the chair opposite and laughing at this unexpected encounter and Kanae keeps her lips stretched, bares her teeth, but she is out of step with his delight, she is watching him from behind the other side of a glass, a thin window settled in the air between them, on his side the joy of running into an old friend, on hers the escape from Alec's appointment, the sound of Alec's voice on her cell phone, and the future she glimpsed when she closed her eyes.

"What are you doing in Komachi?"

"Just business. I can't believe it's you, you're the only person I would have liked to see here and . . . here you are."

"You wrote me lovely letters." She is thinking of the blue paper, the childish stickers and drawings which decorated his letters so many years ago when his family moved away. "I thought you would become an artist."

A memory now on the glass between them, images of their first meeting fifty-five years before when his family moved onto her lonely street, and a stroll in the evening as their parents spoke together for the first time, and an argument between Fumi and his older brothers, settled hastily as Kanae appeared, and then the fireflies rising up as the sun goes down, bleating through the darkness, and Fumi's hands, Kanae's hands, outstretched, together, capturing the creatures and locking them into little glass jars to make a lantern that throbs with light until the insects have no more air and begin to die.

From his side of the glass, Fumikaze is telling her about his family, that his mother is still alive, that his father has passed away, that his brothers have moved up north with their families, that their children are spread around Japan and around the world, and Kanae hears him on her side of the glass and sees that his hair is only mildly gray, that he has aged well, that he wants to hear her own life story and so she gives it, ignoring the ring of the cell phone in her purse, ignoring the white tips of her fingernails as she grips the edge of the table to keep herself from answering that phone, from hearing Alec's voice again.

"You have a family, then?"

"Three children. They are all still on Kyūshū, but none of them live in Komachi."

"Grandchildren?"

"Only one. You?" What matters is listening to this man's story.

Watch the shimmer on the glass between them, watch it waver like it might suddenly vanish. "No. I traveled so much. I never married."

Another memory then, an awkward kiss in the backyard beneath the tree that straddled the line dividing their properties, and the final letters they wrote when Fumi almost told her how he felt and Kanae understood anyway and told him how she felt, which wasn't the same, and then there were no more letters. But now too many years have passed for this to matter so they are back to nothing-talk again, of nieces and travel and Kanae making empty compliments about his traveler's existence and Fumikaze growing outwardly embarrassed but inwardly pleased, and working himself up to the one question that matters and Kanae helping him, finally, needing to mention Alec, to somehow bring him to this table, her only way of saying sorry for leaving him alone at his appointment.

"My husband is from South Africa. My children are only half Japanese."

She is nodding as she says this, angry now, angry for saying something stupid, she has never considered her children half anything, but she cannot take it back, and really it was a gift to Fumikaze because he would not ask until she mentioned it first and now she has, and so of course he wants to know more, he wants to know about Alec and Alec's work because these are questions that must be asked between old friends, but Kanae places her chopsticks down on the table and reaches for her purse, and she looks outside at the cloud of starlings which has swelled to an ocean of black dots, there must be three hundred, four hundred birds, their slender bodies darting and twisting, heady with the tumult and race of their flight.

The words come quickly and she says them, "I'm a widow." She puts this lie between them on the table, breaking the glass wall, and now we know she will leave this restaurant soon, and she will not return to Alec just yet, she will drive back up the mountain to Kurokawa yet again, back to the volcanic waters, to their heat and their sulfur stench, their prickle and scald, and she will pay for a room for the night.

20

霧島

And now for me, yes, it's time, so watch me, too, on this same day, rinsing a tea cup at the sink of this old house, my old house, washing the porcelain beneath the old faucet when I hear the shriek outside and so I drop my cup into the sink and a slender crescent of a chip splits off of the gold-painted lip. I am moving fast to the sliding glass door, scrabbling with the locks and racing out into the yard, taking my cloth bag from the bench by the landing and racing past the shed, out into the back field, looking at the row of thin moss-flecked *sugi* trunks that hems the yard, looking above the crowns of these trees but there is nothing in the sky, nor anything further out above the trees along the ridge of the gorge, until I hear the shriek again, and oh, the poor thing, will I get there in time?

I take the path through the *sugi* and across the back road, over to the trail from the small *onsen* at the bottom of the gorge, and parts of this path are steep, slippery in the damp weather, but my old feet know these trails, my hands know where to reach out for tree roots and stones, steady I climb, steady I keep the river to my left, I am faster than one would expect at my age, but then no one really remembers how old I am anymore. There it goes again, *keeeeeee*— closer now, the bird is losing its voice—how long has it been calling? Why didn't I hear it until now? At the top of the ridge the trees are thick but I know just where to go, because now I hear the hawk with my whole body, the cries are softer now, a stream of harsh chirps that cut through the low hum of the wind rushing through the tree tops, and I walk with my head tilted up, searching the low branches, sunlight from above because this morning's clouds have cleared off, vanished into the lakes that dot these volcanic mountains and my body turns in a slow circle as I move forward, hands stretched out to touch the tree trunks, keeping my balance by gripping the soft red bark with my fingertips.

There! A tall thin pine with peeling bark at the edge of the tree cluster, and on the second to lowest branch the hawk is hunching, one wing flapping at an unnatural angle, its yellow eye watching me, wary, but its cries continue. *Help me. Help me. Help me.*

I am quick and silent, kicking off my shoes and throwing my studded leather belt around the trunk of the tree, and now I am scrambling up the tree like the most agile of our mountain *saru*—I have been able to do this since I was a child, and the cruelest, roughest children on the playground, jealous perhaps, found the taunts that still echo in my ears, dirty monkey, ragged squirrel. I was only thankful they settled on this skill of mine as the reason for their teasing, and knew not much about my family, I am grateful to have suffered so little.

So watch me as I hitch myself up a few more notches, now eye level with the wounded hawk, and I slip a leg over to straddle the branch where he sits, he begins to hop away from me but I am too quick and before he knows what has happened, I have thrown my sack cloth over his head and scooped him up; I wrap him tight, ignoring the high *shrrreeee* of pain as I touch his broken wing, I am sorry, I am sorry, it cannot be helped because the only healing that is painless does not heal.

Bound now, he cannot hurt himself and so I tuck him under one arm, I whisper to him in my secret language while I slide back down the tree, down to the bottom, my bare feet now flat on the ground, soles sticky with pitch and pierced with pine needles and scraped, and I put the bound bird to my chest, let him feel my heartbeat, in his darkness he hears it, a beat, then another: *beat, beat, beat.* He begins to quiet.

"Eh, Kitauchi-san?!"

Turning my head a familiar fear rises and I scan the base of the tree trunks, searching for the flick of a red tail, those amber eyes, but it is only Old Hoshi from the *onsen*, grinning his idiot smile and congratulating me on the hunt, a carton of *shōchū* in his hand and a dirty hat on his head, but before I can even answer him, can tell him I am not hunting, he has already forgotten about me and is weaving his way back toward the trails, my trails, and back toward his room and his family and his bottomless cup of spirits; holding the bird softly against me, I slip back into my shoes and follow Old Hoshi to where the trail forks and as he stumbles off down the right branch, toward the old shrine and the *onsen*, back to his daughter who will scold him and hustle him into his room to sleep off the drink, the bird is jerking beneath my fingers, trying to flap its wings inside its cloth prison, and I am racing along the left branch of the trail, back toward my cages and medicines and wing splints.

Careful, careful now, I say, heading into the shed and hearing the other birds greet me, and the other animals tense in expectation because wild animals in cages are never quiet, never calm, and this newest patient rustles at the sound and the smell of the other creatures. But quickly, quickly I unravel him only to just as quickly set the wing and bind him again and place him into a recovery cage; I have worked for many years to be as fast as I am, the faster I work, the less the animal suffers and he is watching me, blinking those savage yellow eyes, ducking his head and nipping at the gauze, investigating the texture of this material with his beak.

He sneezes against the non-forest smell of his bindings and the shed while I watch him, finding his name, yes, a name is very important, it will be the beginning of his story and so I ask my other patients if we should choose this raptor's name together; only the badger answers with a little yip and so I go to her but when I approach she is backing into a corner, teeth bared, neck-hair bristled because she is still angry with me for not being able to save her cub, and I am angry with me too. But this anger, this red madness between us, will not heal her properly and so we must settle and forgive.

Across the room three hares stare out at me through the mesh of their hutch and I know they will have to go soon, they are ready and every story has a beginning, a middle, and an end, every story's end contains the beginnings of another, and we all know it is time for the hares to begin a new story. I go to the cupboard, this tall cupboard with its six rows of small, box drawers and its large cabinet shelves, built by my grandfather and it is falling apart because Grandfather preferred the ink pot to the hammer, yes, his poetry is never falling apart but this woodwork must be reglued and renailed once a year, a task my grandmother hated, asking me each time why we didn't get our neighbor Endo to help us move it out of the house and into the woodpile.

"Let's burn it, why waste that good wood."

But already then I was old enough to tell *her* what to do, and she could only shake her head and walk away, insulting me as she moved into the next room; I have found no sweetness in this role reversal and so even now that she is gone, and has been gone for so long, she is still able to hold me here, in this house, because by the end we had become too much of the other for me to feel I had any power. It is only in my tasks in this shed, using the medicines left to me by Grandfather and the healing he taught me, and the words, yes he gave me words, and so I push everything the hawk will need through the bars of the cage and he has already started to walk around, he will heal quickly, the raptors always do.

Grandfather almost never took raptors, he said they would heal on their own, he said they knew how to sit perfectly still for weeks at a time, if this was what was needed, and eventually the wing would reknit itself together; I have always doubted this, or maybe I just like being able to hold the power of a raptor between my fingers for those seconds when it is so weak it must submit.

I want to sit with this hawk until I have found his name, but I cannot today because it is time for lessons and the women will be arriving soon—not all of them, today we are missing one, and so I will leave one tea bowl in the cupboard, leave one cake in the box, because Kanae has no time for lessons anymore, her story has no need of my tea ceremony, and I can only hope that my words will still help her and so I check all the cages, touch the animals that will let me and return to the house to clean up my broken tea cup because it will not do for any of the women to think that I have become careless.

霧島

It is evening now in our little town and the winds have settled, for now, for a few hours, while they regroup and gather off shore and over the ocean, preparing for their fury, but for now we are quiet, we can watch the sky and only wonder how it all will come about, and so now Alec is at his home, he has finished his afternoon classes at his little English *juku*, he has walked through town—past the butcher, past the new supermarket, past the garden shop, and past me where I was standing and waiting at the corner for the light to change; he even waved me a quiet hello.

There in his driveway...nothing, Kanae's car has not yet returned, there is nothing but the blurry dark round of the oil stain her car has produced over the last year, and in the kitchen he will find her note, her usual Thursday morning scribble with a promise, yes, a promise, to meet him at his appointment. See him crumple that note now, but he stuffs the little paper ball into his pocket all the same, and now he is at the fridge, now he is pouring a glass of wine because at the hospital they have said nothing about what he may eat and what he must avoid, and because this wine tastes like home and he is fearful that with this everywhere he will soon be nowhere and so he tries to root himself in any way he can.

And this house in our small town is his deepest rooting, despite the years he first lived in another country, despite the memories of his parents and older siblings, all of them gone now except a brother still alive and living in Australia, and there are Christmas cards exchanged and the occasional phone call, but Alec's life has passed here in Komachi, his real life began in fact with the exchange of several sentences at a roadside restaurant, a quick conversation with Kanae and the months that followed of curiosity and love and sex and quick decisions and meeting her parents, of taking her gently away from them and becoming the first version of who he is today.

That man settled into himself with the repetition of a single word, a place name—霧島Kirishima, Kirishima, Kirishima—at night he said this word to himself, the perfectly balanced syllables rising like peaks above a dense mist, because nothing else in Japan had attracted him as much as the image conjured from the delicate characters that made up this word, an island of fog, and inside it, waiting for him, his Kanae.

Now, a lifetime later, he has finished his glass of wine and is pacing the exterior hallway of his house, making a complete circuit of the rooms and continuing for another and then another, and then even another. The Chester house is old, one of the oldest in our town and it has a trademark exterior hallway that once, long ago, allowed servants access to any room without actually ever having to cross from one room to another and when Alec bought the house he called it a balcony and the real estate agent giggled, but now Alec's footfalls on the polished wood are making the house tremble; he is more angry than worried.

Alec stops to brush the leaves of a young gingko tree in its pot by a side door, noting that the plant needs repotting, but for now he only wipes his palm across the broad flat leaves and blows dust into the air which falls like dry rain around his toes, and then he is turning the west corner (for the third time), he is stopping and staring out the windows, watch him now as the muscles in his neck tense with this contemplation of defeat. So soon! And there is steam rising from the vents that dot the far ridge beyond the house, and the steam is uncurling above the greenery and disappearing as it cools.

Now the floor trembles without his taking angry steps; this is how the mountain releases its own tension, little earthquakes, shudders of rock against earth against rock, mild displacements—all reminders of the steam and heat beneath the rocks, beneath our feet.

Alec walks down the stairs and into his garden, he doesn't bother to put on his shoes and when his bare feet hit the paving stones leading into the yard, he feels the little pebbles, the miniature mountains that cut into his feet; this is still his body and it still has feeling—for this he is relieved and his relief comes with little parcels of memory, moments lived in this house, and in this garden.

First a day right here where we are standing, back when he was still filling this garden with plants from his native South Africa, still hoping to grow the grasses and flowers he'd asked his sister to send him, and there, still in his range of inner vision stands Kanae, pregnant with their second child and three-year-old Megumi in a matching homemade sundress and tangled up in her mother's brown legs. In his memory there is sunshine, there is a slowing down of time.

"Those flowers will not grow here," Kanae had said, frowning.
"Sure they will. It's warm enough."
"You are forgetting the winter."
"I'll protect them."
"I'm just warning you, it might not be the same. You might be disappointed."
"I'm happy to try."

And then a quick kiss, the slide of his lips across her cheek and her gentle resistance, because still then, after several years, he could still surprise her with his affection, the spontaneity of it, the lack of concern for anyone who could see, they were outside after all.

But then Megumi was yelling, calling to them from the edge of the garden where she had found a frog hidden in a cluster of grass. *Ashi ga ippon shika nai kono kaeru!* This frog only has one leg! Oh, she screamed and cried, angry or sad they could not tell, but Kanae was already racing to soothe her tears and Alec found the frog and captured it between his fingers. Standing now in his garden, his body silently riddled with this everywhere, he can still feel the frantic one-legged kick of the little creature as it tried to escape his grasp.

Or the time he took his five-year-old son to the jugglers' circus in Miyazaki, just he and Ken'ichi, a man's day out and they ate fried *mochi* and hot *senbei* and Ken'ichi clapped and cried when a little girl balanced on top of ten steel cylinders without slipping or falling down, but then after the show, Ken grabbed Alec's hand and said, "Do not sell Naomi to the circus. Megumi would be okay, but Naomi would never be able to do it." And how he had laughed that night with Kanae, and she laughed as well, until she said to him, just as serious, "But you know he's right. Our Naomi would never be able to do it."

Poor Alec is now jumping up off his bench, jumping up into the purplish light and the heat and fragrance of the flowers, but not in fright or horror at this memory; he is jumping up with hope, at the sound of a foot on their gravel driveway, at the possibility of Kanae's face and the apology he is craving. But it is only Mr. Nishi, their nearest neighbor, and Alec would like to step off into the bushes and hide because he has no energy for this difficult man today.

"Good evening, Chester-san."

And starting from this sentence, Mr. Nishi becomes a human fountain of mundane remarks and run-on words about the weather, about the flowers blooming in Alec's garden, about the density of insects in the air this evening, about another neighbor's new car . . . and Alec knows—we all know—that if Isamu Nishi is not interrupted quickly and politely, he can fill the air with his own breath for up to an hour.

28

"Nishi-san," says Alec, "thank you for the honor of your visit."

"Ah, yes, well, you see . . . hmmm, well, this morning, I . . . uh . . . surely it was my fault, really . . . "

And now it is Alec's turn to smile because he knows that Mr. Nishi means the opposite of this statement, the man is quiet and thoughtful, but he is angry about something and there will be much hemming and hawing now, and Alec must be patient, must keep his temper, must not feel doubly angry now at Kanae's absence because she is usually the one to deal with Mr. Nishi's requests—his complaints over a tree that has tipped a branch too far over the fence, over a toy or a candy wrapper dropped behind in his yard, over a mix-up with the mail or some other service worker.

Finally, in desperation, Alec must try a new strategy and so he says, "Tell me, Nishi-san, what are you saying? My Japanese is so poor, I need you to be direct."

Mr. Nishi straightens in relief—what a surprise!—and says without a single preamble, "Mrs. Chester hit my car this morning. At the stoplight. She let her car roll back into mine. She scraped the bumper. And she didn't even get out to make sure I was okay."

First, silence—our Alec is a little slow to respond—but then his first impulse is to laugh because it is so clear that Mr. Nishi is really only upset that Kanae did not ask after his health, did not get out and spend an hour discussing the accident and how lucky they were that no one really got hurt, how exciting it would have been to call the police and spend some extra minutes looking at the car for scratches!

What a deep fatigue steals over our Alec now, the flat line of his shoulders becomes a curve, the shape of his face sinks in, and he becomes an old man, watch him now, watch the furrows form and the light slink away from his eyes.

"I'm sorry for your trouble, Nishi-san," is all he can say.

But what he really wants to do is weep at the smallness of this man's life, his tiny miserable life with its complaints and neat gray slippers. And here it comes, Alec's first comparison—he is quick to tuck it away but the thought has slipped up unbidden, the horrible question of whether anyone would miss this tiring and ordinary man if Dr. Ishikawa were to give him Alec's everywhere.

But they are already wishing each other good evening and walking in separate directions and the sky is dark now, the insects are beginning to flit about the lamp near the side door to Alec's home, the gnats and the mosquitoes, those striped and furry beasts that will bite him, they always bite him, but he doesn't care, he sits down on the front stoop anyway, because he has always loved this spot, loved watching this driveway and waiting for a visitor, for one of his children to come home from school or for a visit, for Kanae to drive up in high spirits after a lunch with her friends, but he is also sitting now because the shreds of pain have crept up in between his ribs again, his breathing is difficult, his body leaking a cold sweat.

Sweet relief in the ring of his cell phone, in his fumbling fingers to answer the call.

"Naemai?" he is whispering, this invented name, his only endearment for her, another hybrid of his life before and his life now: Kanae, my *ai*. Kanae, my love.

Silence . . . then crackles and static, and he waits, he cannot hang up, hearing her in the empty twitch of electricity and space.

When the silence is again too much, Alec stands and steps backward into the house, into his house with its porch and roof and windows, such a solid structure, and he thinks of the *kanji* for window—窓 —with its three seemingly unconnected root pictographs: space,

30

I, heart—and he sees it for the first time, like a student again, this *I* like a person wedged between an open space and a heart, like a man standing still, his heart wedged and painful, looking out onto the open sky.

霧島

Summer evenings on southern Kyūshū retain their light for an eternity, clutch it bundled high above the island with bands of color and breezes from the not-so-far sea, and the sun hangs over the ridge of the mountains, like a wild eye bearing down on the little town of Komachi and the rest of the towns and villages of our Fog Island Mountains. Beneath this sun, Kanae has now said good-bye to her old friend Fumikaze and is driving back up the little mountain road for the third time today—this is when she sees the gathering of the cloud ocean, something she hasn't seen for years, although it is what makes our region famous throughout Japan.

She is slowing the car down; what else can she do on this first evening of her flight? She is only interested in slowing time and so she pulls over to a scenic lookout and stands with her hands against the low rock wall, watching the mist gather first over the treetops, slowly, collecting its white weight in billowing folds, and she is staring at this thick whiteness and her hand is reaching out into the void as if she might be able to touch the millions of droplets that are creating the vapor of this foggy ocean.

If we are quiet, if we are careful, we, too, can watch this ocean amass. *Shhh*, we are just behind her, we are writing her and we are aware that in a few minutes these clouds will look so solid, so thick, that Kanae might think she could actually walk off the ledge and walk across them, because of course she knows the story of the young girl from Matsuzaki who did this. It is a story my grandfather wrote in one of his longest poems, and his version or older ones are still told at festivals and in children's books. Kanae read it to her children and it always made Megumi clap and dance and it is this she is thinking about, she is seeing her own daughter jump across the white mist, like the young girl from so long ago who was sent out by a jealous older sister into a dark and dangerous forest to gather mushrooms, and who was chased by a wild boar and almost fell off the cliff to the rushing river and rocks below, but no, the cloud sea held her aloft and she walked to safety across the void to the other mountain ridge.

Of course no one knows what happened to her on the other side. Not even my grandfather.

But now Kanae is back inside the car, driving slowly through the now dense fog, the higher she climbs the more fog settles across the road, and the blazing eye of the sun is virtually lost to her now down amid the cloud sea, and she must turn on her fog lights because everything is muted now, white and wispy, and she drives past a deer grazing along the side of the road; it only runs away at the last second when it finally hears her approach.

She is turning on her windshield wipers to erase the gathered condensation across the glass, and in the flick of her wrist is the first gesture of her anger, but she is already tamping it down, closing her eyes and pressing on the gas pedal. There is a curve ahead but she knows this road by heart, and so she takes a deep breath and her eyes are still closed; she pictures the curve and turns the steering wheel to match her memory and now she is pressing even harder on the accelerator, still steering by instinct and there is a rush of sound in her ears—is it her? Is she yelling?

But the car lurches over something and her eyes fly open. There is no use checking the rear view mirror, she is going too fast and the fog is too thick and so she is telling herself it was probably a fallen branch, or perhaps a mountain toad, but it doesn't matter, she is refusing to be moved at the possible death of a small animal because she is exactly where she thought she would be, she has negotiated the curve in her blindness.

At the *onsen* the staff members are surprised to see her return yet again and they are silent as she pays for their smallest room, a Western style closet without even a window, and she can smell the grease and the fish from the kitchens even if the bathroom is immaculately clean. She removes her shoes and lies down on the single bed, but then she is standing and getting undressed, shivering in the slight chill of this early evening, and she wraps herself in the cotton robe provided by the hotel and slips out toward the baths, shuffling along in slippers that are much too large for her slender feet.

There in the sound of her *shuffle shuffle shuffle* along the carpet comes a memory of her mother, and Kanae is remembering how, toward the end of her mother's life, she had to help her along this very hallway, help her to these very baths, and how her mother could not keep the slippers on her feet and kept flinging them forward with each step, only to have to scramble toward them and slip her feet again into the soft brown plastic; each time she flicked a slipper, she would lower her head in shame, shuffle gracelessly forward and struggle to place a shaking foot where it belonged.

Kanae, with her but unwilling to really help her, would watch her mother's shame and grow irritated, she would step ahead and hold the door to the baths in a gentle reproach of her mother's slow progress, because Kanae knew that everyone had trouble with these oversized and unsuitable *onsen* slippers, everyone in every *onsen* across Japan, so why couldn't her mother laugh about it? Why couldn't she shrug her shoulders and say, "It can't be helped!"

But now Kanae is pulling open that *onsen* door for herself and feels only the lingering glance of her fragile mother from the empty hallway, and the changing room is empty and she knows the baths might be empty too, and so she almost turns back around because she does not trust herself to be alone tonight in the baths, with all that heated water, all that possibility of oblivion; the sound of someone moving about in the pools is reassuring and Kanae undresses carefully and heads through the sliding glass door.

At the threshold she sees the old woman standing beneath the bamboo pipe waterfall at the far end of the large bath, and she thinks of her mother and her mother's death and then Alec is with her again, and the anger flares, there it is in the swift judging glance she gives to this woman's sagging breasts and fat belly, there it is again in the violent grip she uses to carry her stool and bucket over to the showers, and there it is in the icy water she sprays against her shoulders and down along her neck. She lets the water run until her teeth are chattering, until her skin is blue, and then she walks over to the bath and steps in as quickly as she can, wanting the shock of the heat against her frozen skin, wanting the pain of it to rise up against her rage.

Tropical Depression

It is morning now and he is back again, and waiting still, but this time the hospital has prepared Alec a special room and still he is surprised, even after so many years, he knows he should be upstairs, in the same wing with the other Komachi men; instead someone has cleaned out one of the older, larger rooms on the first floor, rolled in a bed and put up new curtains. Alec is looking at these curtains, at their strange brightness, and he is thinking that one of the nurses has brought them in from her home, he is thinking it might be Nurse Uchida, because she is one of his students and she has always liked him, but he is also wondering why he should be treated any differently than anyone else and he wants to be angry about this, he wants to feel a sense of outrage, indignation. But nothing comes, he has accepted (and it's good that he has) that foreigners in small-town Japan remain foreign, even after several decades.

A nurse is coming in now and she asks if he's comfortable and he says yes and they exchange a number of quiet sentences that have no meaning, little barren phrases that could make Alec angry—it's always lurking, the line of a temper—if he had the energy, but instead he is looking at the small room and the extra chair and square table, these items a courtesy for visitors. For Kanae. For Kanae who did not come home in the night, who was an empty space in their bed for the six hours of troubled sleep Alec allotted himself until the smell of their sheets, of her, of his own pillow, was too much, and so he got up and paced the house until it was time to pack his small bag for the hospital and walk across town.

Alec is now arranging the sheet and thin blanket over his legs as though their slight weight might put a lid on his surge of despair, and he thinks only that the hospital is too cold, and that this is something he can fix so he slides gently out of bed—already he is taking too much care with his body, moving like an invalid—and he opens the window to let in some of the heat and the damp.

"You'll cost us a fortune," says Dr. Ishikawa, who has put on his most cheerful face. "The air conditioner in the next room will start working overtime."

"The Japanese have never understood a happy medium."

"We like a challenge."

"You want everything perfect, but you go too far. You torture trees, Shingo. You want to control nature."

Ishikawa is shaking his head, smiling, smiling and sad because he is very attached to this man, this friend from another country, but today he must be a doctor and not a friend because they have a series of tests and they have already scheduled Alec's surgery for the afternoon; an exploratory surgery, with the possibility of growth removal if possible and he is explaining all this to Alec when Nurse Uchida enters the room, a nod for the doctor, a deeper bow for Alec, and she leaves and comes back immediately pushing a wheelchair.

"This is ridiculous," Alec is sputtering. "No, no, I'm fine, I can walk."

"It is customary."

"I'm really fine. I'll feel better on my feet."

"Please. I am more stubborn than you, Alec. Please."

A thought strikes—in all the years that Alec has lived in Komachi, and for all his family's mishaps: Ken's broken arm, Naomi's pneumonia, and Kanae's three pregnancies, he himself has never been a patient at the hospital, never overnight, never like this, never a serious accident or illness, and so it occurs to him that he has led an exceptionally healthy life, and it also occurs to him that someone has been keeping track and now it is his turn to pay up.

"How self-centered of you," Kanae would say. "This is Western thinking."

And she would be right, and so Alec closes a fist over the arm of the wheelchair and leans back into the sticky plastic, letting it all go, for now, and oh, how I wish she were wrong, Alec, I really do, for then I could write a villain into your poem and we, all of us together, would be able to chase him away.

The conversation is growing intense now between these three as Dr. Ishikawa and the nurse lead Alec through scans and X-rays, through an examination of his entire body—slender fingers palpating and touching and measuring and feeling. For the first time in years there is a question of vocabulary, he's never had to learn the Japanese words for these tricky medical terms and so they bring out a dictionary and every-one makes a big show of how educational this is, as if understanding the term for metastatic lesion—*tenisō*, such a soft-sounding killer— means nothing more to any of them than passing an upcoming test.

Finally, finally, it is late morning and he rests, or at least he is pre-tending, because he is also dialing Kanae's cell phone once again, and there is no answer and he wonders, hopes really, that she has spoken to their children.

Which brings him to a deep breath and the idea that he must do this himself, he must do this because the line of speech must remain drawn through his family, regardless of Kanae, they must not forget their children—haven't they already done this too much?—and already his fingers are dialing, already he is listening to the phone ring through and then it comes, the gentle tenor of Ken'ichi, the youngest, his only son.

"Father, I was just about to call you, is it serious?"

Relief that Kanae has not left their children, too, and relief at the sound of his son's voice because Ken'ichi will understand exactly what it all means, he will not have to say more than necessary with Ken'ichi; already Ken is concerned that Alec should be moved to a larger hospital in Fukuoka or Kagoshima, somewhere they might have newer, and by this he means, *better*, radiotherapy treatments.

"They know what to do here. I'm in good hands."
"What is happening first?"
"I'm having surgery this afternoon. An investigation. Then we'll know more."
"I'm coming. Can Mother get me at the station?"

Alec manages calm, manages to be firm, despite the rising panic, and he is insisting that no one rush, that there is nothing to be so frightened about, and that they'll know what to do after today's results, and he is also thinking that maybe this evening Kanae will come back and he will not be forced to lie to his children about not knowing where to find their mother.

Ken is not the kind of son to bully and push, he will accept Alec's decision in the same way he accepts all of the decisions made without his consent; for this Kanae has always called him our Japanese son, the one who truly understands the words tradition and duty, but Alec does not agree, has never agreed, because Ken reminds him of his own maternal grandfather, a farmer from Rhodesia who loved nothing more than to watch the sun rise up over the veld from his front porch, a man with an immense collection of spider lilies, wisteria, and dombeya, a man quiet with his responsibilities and careful never to cause upset.

"I must return for my tests. I'll be in touch later today."

Ken's silence is a cold one, a space of time stretched out with a frustration that Ken will not openly reveal to his father, but Alec is cutting it short, already hanging up and aware, with a tight breath, aware that now is when he will pay the price for loving Kanae more than he loved his children—he never meant to do this because no one plans on that sort of thing.

More knocking on the door, the slender figure of Nurse Uchida with her long hair and wide eyes, and she is moving about the bed, rustling these stiff white sheets and snapping his pillow, smoothing the blanket at the foot of his bed, and she keeps moving until she is far enough away from him to face him directly and then she stands, strict and still.

"It is none of my business." She is rearranging the towels and bathrobe hanging from a hook on the bed post. "It is none of my business, but Sensei should be honest with Mrs. Chester."

The laughter is up out of his throat before he can stop it and he lets it roll across the length of his legs stretched out on this bed, lets it shake his torso until he must suck in his breath at the pain of the movement, because now he understands why the staff members have been giving him guarded glances and half-started sentences—it is all so horrifically funny. For the first time in his life in Japan, he is being credited with truly Japanese behavior.

"I haven't lied to Mrs. Chester."

"She should be here with you."

"Oh, I couldn't agree more."

And there it is, the flash of panic in her eyes, the fear that she will somehow disappoint him, he has seen it many times before during their English lessons—she is not comfortable with sarcasm, is much too afraid to misunderstand.

"Uchida-san, I've been trying to get a hold of her. She knows, I believe, exactly what is going on."

The pity in her eyes vanishes almost instantly, but Alec has seen it, has felt it and it has made him ugly, made him shrink into himself, away from her, and he just wishes she would go now, would leave him be, because he's always enjoyed her company during their lessons, enjoyed her curiosity about his life before he came to Japan and his life as a foreigner in their midst, but he can no longer look at her and she is backing up, backing away, making her excuses and finding comfort in the polite phrases and formulas of good-bye and take care.

霧島

This morning the *onsen* is nearly busy—five old women, ancient creatures with wrinkled bellies and gray hair who are meandering back and forth from the outside bath to the sauna to the inside bath to the showers and around and around, their naked bodies circulating in the steam and the heat, they walk together, they call to one another, they laugh at each other's jokes; except for polite greetings, they leave Kanae alone but she cannot leave them, cannot keep her eyes from watching them, she is studying their movements from beneath the veil of water at the shower, from beneath the small towel she piles upon her head while she sits in the inside bath, from her stance at the bamboo waterfall she watches them and instead of relaxing in this hot water and this steam, she grows more and more rigid, her arms tighten, her shoulders tense, her jaw becomes a set line across her cheek.

She is shaking now as she stands up out of the bath and walks into the changing room, she has difficulty buttoning her blouse, difficulty zipping up her jeans and she is almost away from this room, away before the older women finish their bathing, but the old ladies are too quick and they are coming into the room now, discussing someone's daughter and giggling, or asking questions about the stain on a kimono and arguing about how to get it clean, and so Kanae hustles a retreat into the restroom stall, and there it comes up—her entire breakfast, barely digested, rice and salmon and egg, little clods of seaweed stick to the porcelain and she is coughing and spitting, wiping at her forehead.

"Are you all right in there?"
"Oh, that doesn't sound good."
"Say, can we get you anything?"

Kanae thanks them for their trouble but she cannot open the door to look at their creased lonesome faces, she will not do it, she sits on the floor instead, resting her face against the toilet seat and she heaves again but there is nothing left in her stomach and she can only clutch her stomach at the pain of it, spit some acid into the bowl.

"She's not fainted, has she?"
"She didn't look well in the bath."
"Hmm, *sō da nē*, maybe it's her heart."
Kanae yells through the door that she is fine, that she's just a little tired.
"There's a stomach flu going around. My grandson told me. You sure you don't have that?"

"Yes, everyone is sick, it's this weather, it holds the germs."
"No," Kanae whispers, "I'm in perfect health."

Standing now, closing her eyes, she buttons and unbuttons her blouse, she smooths the sleeves, she swallows back the vomit taste on her tongue, and then she is unlocking the door, rushing through the mob of widows—she couldn't stand it if they were to touch her—and she gathers the rest of her clothing, she will not stay here among them. She is bowing without looking at them, thanking them for their concern, and then she is out, breathing again in the quiet hallway, but halfway to her room she realizes she is still wearing the toilet slippers and she must go back, but no, she can't, her feet will not walk in that direction, and so she must kick them off in the hallway, ashamed at this behavior, and run the rest of the way to her room.

Poor Kanae will find no peace today, already her cell phone is beeping at her with a message, and she is sitting down to listen to it, bare feet dangling over the edge of the bed and biting on a hangnail that has ripped halfway down her thumb; as she listens to Alec's voice and his explanation, his tidy anger, she pulls harder on the little flap of skin and it is tearing slowly, a little drop of blood rises, but the pain seems to be happening to someone else.

"Just call the hospital and they'll tell you what room I'm in."
Silence.
"They've put me in a special room. It's so strange. You'll see."
Silence.
"Please, *Naemai*..."

Her thumb is bleeding now and she sucks on it, greedily, finding a thrill in the dark metal taste of her own blood on her tongue and throat.

In ten minutes she has dressed, paid her bill and is seated back inside her car, and she will go straight to the hospital, because what on earth has she been thinking, she has not been herself, she is being ridiculous, she must do her duty to Alec—and then it stops her, this idea that he might be frightened, that he might not have understood something, that he might have needed to ask her a question, because it has been years since she really needed to act as a buffer between her husband and their home, years since she needed to explain an expression to him, or someone's behavior, but she sees now that this is what her job must be, this is where she is failing him, and she presses harder on the accelerator, grips the steering wheel with both hands.

Outside the morning sun is shining, not a trace of the cloud sea and only a hint of the storm to come, this hint in a heaviness around us, a tense vibration in the air, and so Kanae is driving carefully, she is not speeding, she is holding her car steady in her lane, and she watches for deer and other animals, she even slows down at each tanuki-crossing sign, careful and apologetic; halfway down she passes a school bus and suddenly her own children, not the adults they are now but the ghosts of their childhood selves, are in the car with her, Ken'ichi in the middle between his two sisters, always the quiet one, always watching out the window over Naomi's shoulder, never over Megumi's who would have pushed him back, told him he was crowding her. Kanae hears them now, their innocent childish babble, about the food they would want to eat once they got home or about their friends at school, and she is amazed to remember how her children always kept their conversations to themselves, they never shouted at her and solicited her to join in, and she never knew this was strange until a friend once mentioned that she couldn't get a moment of peaceful reflection in the car because her children were too busy interrupting her, asking for her attention, needing her to comment on their own conversations.

"Mine hardly speak to me. They talk amongst themselves!"
"Oh, how lucky you are!"

Yes, she had thought so too, at the time, but now she wonders, straining her ear backward to hear the whispers of their ghosts, why they never wanted her to join in, why didn't they ask her? Why didn't they need her more?

The hospital parking lot is nearly empty this morning but Kanae pulls up along the street instead, she parks her car but before she can get out, she is heaving again, stretching a hand for her purse, for a tissue, anything, a piece of paper, something to catch the stomach juices that heave up out of her mouth and into her lap, and now it's done and she is panting against the steering wheel, her stomach constricted and dry, and she has slightly peed her pants with the force of her retching; there was nothing to get rid of, but her body wouldn't believe her.

She does not dare look at the hospital again—all those windows, all those doors. Automatic doors just ready to open for her, willing to sense her arrival and slide right open, to welcome her back into her life and the days to come that cannot be stopped from coming upon her, and so again, she stays where she is, she starts the car and then turns it off, she folds her hands carefully together and waits until they have stopped shaking, and she puts her head down because she is certain that no one can see her, she has parked so carefully behind a big truck and in the shade of an enormous tree, and so I wonder if I should go to her, should I walk over and knock against the glass of her car window and ask her if I could help, could I give her my arm to walk with her into the hospital, would this be enough? But it is too late already, she has started the car again and she is pulling out onto the street too quickly, her tires screeching and her mouth twisted and her eyes determined and we know that she is not yet ready.

No matter, I am already late and the children will be getting restless, especially with this heat, and so I hurry along the sidewalk, fanning myself because I am sometimes a lazy old woman and my bag of puppets has grown heavy this morning, just a bit more up this hill, past the hospital and the Italian restaurant and toward the elementary school, and a quick glance to the sky—we have some time yet, those clouds are heavy but they are not yet filled with spite—and off I go, one more building, and then I see it, and the children are waving to me from the window and the young mothers are smiling and the teacher is waving her hand and so I must smile and bow and here I am.

"Good morning, Azami Bā-san!"

Their voices are so cheerful and their faces shining in this heat, with their excitement, they know I will make them laugh, I will make them cover their eyes in fright, especially young Inokida-kun, who is afraid of everything, and he will hide behind his sister and his mother will swat him gently on the head with her paper fan because she wants him to be brave, for her own sad reasons she needs a son who will fight, and so I will change one of my stories for him, I am already rewriting it in my head, because the clever thing with stories is that they are never really fixed, they are meant to change as often as the listener needs them to be something else entirely.

Some of the children are too hot, their faces pink and sweaty, their little mouths open and their eyes rolling around the room, they would like to ask their mothers for a juice box or an ice cube, they would like to remove their clothing and dance about this library in bare feet and naked bodies, but the mothers are impatient for the story, impatient for the moment when their children no longer need them, all eyes on me, all hands gripped in their laps, and so I begin, I am not even kneeling on the floor before the children, but already there is a puppet on my hand, a long and sparkly snake and quickly, from behind my back, the snake takes a frog up into its mouth and is about to devour it, and the children are laughing, because my snake is a sharp and funny creature, a jokester, but wait—here comes a woman, a painted paper bag over my other hand, and she is begging the snake to give the frog his freedom, but he won't listen, he is very stubborn, and so she tries again, she promises to become his wife, and the children are screaming, what a horrible thought, for who would want to marry a snake?

I tell them stories of crabs and fish, of clever mermaids and simpler stories of boys and girls who speak and think much like they do, and little Inokida-kun is watching me because we are about to come to his favorite part, to the best story of them all, and all the children know I will finish my storytelling hour with the biggest, brightest most beautiful puppet, and when I bring her out, there is always a lovely silence, even the teacher and the librarian are nodding and smiling and waiting for me to begin, and so I ask them.

"Now who is this?"
"KI—TSU—NE!" There was not even a pause, this word has been bubbling up inside them since I came into this room.

Oh how they love to say this name, and they yell it again and again, and their lips are shining a little and their eyes are growing rounder and even the mothers who have been chattering away at the back of the room have put down their tea cups and turned away from their complaints and advice and have come forward for this final story.

"And how many tails does she have?"

The children are raising their hands and trying to get to their feet, one of them will be allowed to come forward and count the fox's tails, and today I think it will have to be Inokida-kun because he has not hidden behind his sister even once. I call him forward and at first he doesn't want to come, but his mother is helping him, her eyes greedy to touch the puppet, and I must turn my body to keep her from it—it is only for the children, only their fingers are worthy to feel Kitsune's grace.

46

He is counting now, caressing each red tail, and then he smiles when he touches the last one. "Nine!"

And all of the children know that a nine-tailed fox is the wisest of them all, that she has lived the longest life, has earned her powers, and she can hear any conversation, she can see any person by just closing her eyes and thinking about them, and she can travel through the air and vanish back again with only a blink, she is nearly a goddess and while we love her fiercely, we are also all a little afraid of her and so Inokida-kun and his mother have seen that it is time and they are backing away and ready for the sound of my voice.

The children know this tale and the mothers do too, so it is easy to pull a kimono over the head of the puppet and then take the young man puppet from my bag and jump right to the middle of the story when the fox has already taken human shape and tricked the young man on that lonely deserted road, it was so easy you see, because she was young and beautiful, and the children are clapping because they love the wedding dance and the song the fox-woman is singing to her beloved, and soon there is a little baby nestled inside the front fold of her kimono and the children are chanting *aka-chan! aka-chan!* and everyone is smiling because the story makes us happy. But then one of the children makes the sound of a dog barking, knowing that soon enough the couple's life will be disturbed by the puppy who doesn't like its mistress and so soon we are all yipping a little and even the old librarian is laughing at the excitement in our little corner of this building, and then the fox-woman is begging her husband to get rid of the dog and the children are sad and the mothers are shaking their heads, but we should never doubt him, because of course the husband won't agree, this is a good and faithful little dog, and everyone is cheering... until I begin to measure my words, and my voice grows deeper because we are coming to the final day when the fox-woman is taking her husband his lunch in the fields with her little boy toddling next to her and the little dog is yipping, yapping at her heels and this time it takes a little bite, just a snip at her ankles, it can't help it, it has waited for so long, and the fox-woman jumps, startled at the feel of these dog teeth on her ankle, and before she can stop herself she has turned back into a fox and raced away over the hedge and the young man and his child are left staring at the woods.

"No! No! No! She comes back! She comes back!"

Yes, I tell them, of course she comes back, because she was a good wife and a good mother and so every night she transforms back into a woman and the husband has missed her, and he tells her to stay, just for the nights, he is the one to name her, Kitsune, and it means "come and sleep, come and sleep," and the family is happy again and so the children are clapping, they have forgotten the heat of the storm and their noontime hungry bellies, but all good fun must come to an end, so I am removing the puppet and becoming myself again, and the mothers are thanking me and the children have come forward, just an inch, wanting to touch me, and I kneel to them and wink at their little faces, and then it is time to go and the librarian tells me that Monday's story hour is cancelled, on account of the storm, and I am nodding and leaving and walking back down the hill, back past the restaurant and the hospital, and there are so many people walking in and out of those sliding glass doors, and maybe I could go in and talk to Alec, give him a few minutes of my time today, but no, he is surrounded, there are too many people watching him now, so I keep up my slow little pace and I check that Kitsune's nine tails are safely tucked away, and I can't help it, I keep my hand on them, thrust deep into my bag, because this redness, this softness, will carry me home.

霧島

All these sounds beyond the door, these signs of life in our hospital—the phrases of conversation that drift through to him, the laughter of a nurse and the grim embarrassed cough of a doctor who must give bad news to a mother about the reason for her child's bloody nose, all of this is settling in on our Alec, curving around him and weaving its way into his mind to become a part of his story, because how can it not. Here is a man who has made integration into Komachi a kind of life's work; from the moment of his marriage he wanted nothing but acceptance from all of us and he forced himself upon this little community in his tall tender way and he has followed our rules and laughed at us when we struck him as odd, but never unkindly, because he has always known that he has wanted us more than we needed him, and he has even added to our number with his three children, and then taught our children, on evenings and weekends, and taught our uncles and our wives and our daughters, he has taught them the words they will need if they ever want to leave this place, and so we have loved him in return, we have almost taken him for one of us, and as soon as it becomes known—the news is already traveling around, among his students, among the neighbors, and this is such a small town really—that he is in the hospital and that the outlook is not good, there will be a worried hush and a ripple of fear, and people will begin to pay attention, will want to stop in to see him, to bring him careful gifts and sound advice. Already today there is a woman on her way in, ready to ask about him at the front desk, a former student, a woman in her seventies whose life wish had been to travel to America and see about locating the daughter of a long-lost sister, one of those women who married a piece of paper and vanished away on a boat, and this old woman wanted, more than anything, to be able to speak enough English before she went and Alec was happy to help her.

Luckily she will not get past the front desk because Alec will already be in surgery by the time she gets here, but she will tell one of the receptionists to send wishes to Mrs. Chester and the receptionist's face will go quiet and her eyes will look down, but still she will lean in closer to the window and right there, right then, this afternoon, the rumor will begin and before the end of the day,

Komachi will be wondering why Kanae has not set foot inside the town hospital.

For now Alec is still safe from this concern, he is sitting rather stiffly in his hospital room fingering his cell phone and wondering if it was a mistake to leave such a long message on Kanae's cell phone, but what else could he do, whatever she thinks she knows might not be what is really happening, at least this is what Alec would like to think, and his fingers tap the screen of the phone, dialing her number again, erasing it, dialing it, erasing it, what's done is done, he's told her; putting the cell phone to the side, he makes himself watch the television but really he is wondering what it will be like to be opened up today, to have the surgeon's gloved fingers wielding that knife and slicing through his skin, inserting a camera that will roam around inside his middle with its electronic eyes and its tiny cable, sneaking past the muscley walls of his stomach to get a look at his diseased pancreas, and Alec knows this little camera will be looking for all the abnormal cells and measuring the size of the tumors and sending back the data that will help them all make some kind of guess about just how much longer he has to live.

And he can't help it, he has always had an interest in science and so he is placing a hand across his belly and wishing he could know what it all looks like, how are the organs touching and where are the growths, how much blood will there be, and will those tumors be big, and really, what he truly wants to know is what it all looks like right now, this instant, when his body is still intact, when not a single light particle has touched the tissues of his inner belly, and so what color is the pancreas when there is no one there to look at it? And then he smiles, not a real smile but a baring of teeth, because here is maybe the only time he will appreciate the power of a koan, here is the only paradox he will want to ponder for hours and maybe if he just thinks about it long enough, if he tries his hardest to sort this one out, maybe, just maybe, he'll find that there isn't anything to worry about after all.

"Don't you think it's funny," he is saying now, into the empty room.

He likes the sound of his voice but he lowers his volume to a whisper in order to feel safer from the intrusions beyond his hospital door, and he continues on, saying everything he is thinking out loud until suddenly he is deep in conversation. With himself. With his wife. With his doctor. With God and Buddha and Nature. With his children. It's all there and he is almost proud of the way that he keeps calm, at the questions he can ask without trembling, at the way the roll of words and breaths and pauses are covering this empty space of this afternoon. Yes, Alec, you are good at waiting . . . *shōshō omachi kudasai.*

Soon enough he drifts away, he has said enough, he has ticked off the questions that will never have answers from his long fingers, shoved them beneath the folds of the little blanket on his lap and he can watch his television show again without really seeing it, just listening to the sounds of the Japanese words and the laughter of the game host in his plaid hat and his laughing eyes and the perfect faces of the young contestants with their shiny hair and glossy lips and this is all a comfort, this media perfection and the shouts of the audience when someone gets an answer wrong but has said something funny. This is his home. This is his home. This is his home.

When the anesthesiologist arrives with a male nurse and a closed-down face, they do not speak to him right away, they take his temperature and examine the color of his eyes, but their busy silence is unnerving and so Alec smiles at them and says in his kindest voice that he is ready and they grunt—not unkindly—their agreement and so they help him onto a gurney and take him into a room for washing the germs from the skin of his belly, and the male nurse has the softest hands, his touch is like a caress, and Alec is amazed, nearly embarrassed, but then they are giving him a pill to relax him—although he is already far too relaxed, too willing to submit—and they ask him a single, simple question.

"Nani mo tabete nai desu yo ne?"

But he has heard another verb, a verb that sounds similar, he has heard something about being bundled up, or tying up, and he doesn't really understand, so he tells them, "No, I have not bundled up, but will it be cold during the surgery?"

There is uncomfortable laughter and Alec sees immediately that he has misunderstood the most simple of questions, because of course he was not allowed to eat before his surgery and they will want to be sure of this before giving him any anesthesia, and so, no longer relaxed but ashamed, because his Japanese is far better than this, he explains his mistake and everyone is relieved and there are jokes about putting his hair into a bun, what a lovely style for sensei, oh ho ho, and one of the men says, suddenly serious, that the women are lucky really, because this weather is so hot, and wouldn't he love to get his hair off his brow, and suddenly we are all thinking about the storm because it is still coming, and those winds are picking up again, and it is now only a matter of hours before the typhoon will reach us here on Kyūshū.

霧島

Kanae holds herself at attention within the enclosed capsule of her car, speeding now along the wide freeway, away from our town, following the dark ribbon cut through the mountains of this volcanic island, through tunnels and over rivers, past the walls of trees and concrete built up to hold back landslides. She is escaping to the north, away from us and toward the ocean, toward Kumamoto, toward her daughter and her grandson, because this is a legitimate reason to keep herself away from Komachi today. The radio is on but Kanae is not listening—she is rigid, hands on the steering wheel, back so straight it has begun to ache, her eyes straining to see the next road sign, the next exit; they are few and far between but she is counting them one after the other and calculating the minutes between each possible exit as her car hums and races always forward, as far away from Komachi as possible, until she reaches the place she wants, Yatsushiro.

But she is interrupted by the chirp of her cell phone and she must pull off and let it ring through because she is not going to answer this one, she is only going to stare at the name that has flashed across the display and then close her eyes, wait for the ringing to stop. And when it does she clicks through to get the message and Alec's voice is nearly too strong, too real for her, but she listens, she has to, and she gets the whole story, she gets this word everywhere and now it is hers as well. There is more though and it's his forgiveness, which is already too much, he knows that she is afraid and he admits that he is too, but he reminds her that he needs her, that she is being selfish, and here she hangs up quickly because all she wants to tell him is that her being selfish is beside the point, because he is the one going to leave her all alone.

Yes, Yatsushiro, where the Kuma River leaks into the Yatsushiro Sea and she must slow down and turn to the right, still heading north but now on a smaller road, with the ocean off to her left somewhere behind the buildings, but the mass of it has changed the air here, she is no longer in the mountains, and she takes a deep breath and then another and all that salt water smell goes down too smoothly and she is greedy for it.

Because here is her grandson and her daughter already, outside their little apartment building in this southern suburb of Kumamoto, and she is waving and honking her little horn, playing the harebrained grandmother who is running late, and of course she was planning to come today, of course she is sorry, and yes, they should hurry up into one car to make it to the dojo on time. But first she must swoop up her little Jun and swing him around and feel the sturdy little bones of his arms and legs and try to keep the teeth away from her joy at the touch of his arms wrapped around her neck, but she can't, she is squeezing him too tight and already he is wriggling away.

"Shouldn't you be with Dad?"
"I won't do anyone any good by sitting around the hospital worrying. They're running tests. We'll know more tonight what is happening."

As she speaks she must breathe quickly, as the bile rises in her throat again, as this ugliness inside her threatens to spill out and she pants slowly, rushing Jun into his car seat with her head down, her hands clutching at him, patting his hair, touching his cheek, wanting to steal away some of his innocence and health.

"Well, you're here, Mother—better get in. We're going to be late. As usual."
Looking at her daughter now, looking outside of herself for the first time in days and there's a surprise in this, the world filled with its own events. "You look exhausted."
Megumi laughs and says in English, "Ten points for Mum!"

A family joke, a phrase Alec gave to their family when the children were young, when they'd managed some difficult task and he would lift them to the sky and shout, "A hundred points for you!" And then later, when they were in school and brought home good marks, the same phrase was trotted out and laughed over and only Megumi would turn their family joke into something sarcastic.

"I am just worried. Are you all right?"
"We're all worried."
Only Megumi would turn her mother's concern around and make it about something else.

So they speak of nothing—of the weather and the pressure changes and the chance that the storm will come soon, of the rain they have predicted for the afternoon and that Kanae should be careful when she drives back to Komachi; they talk about Jun and his daycare schedule and about Megumi's old car and whether it will last through the end of the year because it is sputtering about and threatening total breakdown.

In this sideways, oblong way, this mention of decay, they have brought Alec's illness into the car and Kanae can no longer breathe, can no longer think, can only roll down her window and stick her head outside and the shame rolls off of her as her stomach retches again but nothing comes out and the other cars are looking at her and Megumi is taking in a swift, angry breath and Jun is wondering out loud if Grandma needs a tissue.

"Ken said it was serious," Megumi says quickly, her words clipped and quiet.

Kanae holds her breath. She stops time. She doesn't blink. She doesn't move.

"Ken wants to move Dad to a bigger city. To a place where the treatments might be different."

"This is beside the point."

Thankfully, they are now pulling into the parking lot and herding Jun into the building with the other three-years-olds, each of them tottering beneath the weight of their practice *kendōgi*, and Megumi watches for a short while and Kanae is beside her, listening to the grunts and laughter of the children as they race across the mats and bow to each other and follow the instructions of their teacher with happy chatter and small physical feats.

But Megumi is pulling her quickly outside, already holding a cell phone to her ear, already in conversation with her younger sister—and Kanae is frozen, picturing her middle child, her sweet and clumsy Naomi, whose eyes were blue at birth and only darkened to hazel, whose secrets are stashed away in her shy, guarded heart, whose fragility frightens them all.

Kanae walks away from this conversation between her two daughters, walks into a space, just a few feet away, where what is happening to her belongs only to her; she steps past a low gate and into a playground and there she watches a mother and a child, watches the little boy poke his mother in the kneecap with a little stick, his eyes are mischievous and the mother is protesting, she is making a stern face, she is calling him naughty, but the little boy won't be dissuaded, he is poking again and giggling and making up a story, and soon the mother is chasing him away, part of his story, laughing and happy, and despite the wind that is thickening around them all there is sunshine on this playground and Kanae hopes it will stay.

Megumi is beside her again, a hand on her arm and Kanae is trying to keep what is happening under control.

"Listen . . . Megu-chan . . . I . . . we still need to talk to the doctor."
"It's Ishikawa?"
Kanae nods.
"Well, Ishikawa will know what is best, he is Dad's friend, he will—"
"Megu, there is no best."

But her voice is starting to sound hysterical and she closes it off, she silences herself and coughs, she turns back to this mother and her child, she turns away from her own child because she should never have come, she should have driven south this morning, caught a plane, left the country, left the planet.

"What does Dad say?"

Kanae is staring out at the busy road, counting the cars as they slide past her eyes, reds and whites and blacks, the glint of chrome in the tiny ray of sunlight still peeking through the darkening clouds, and are those the first drops of rain? Kanae says something to Megumi but she says it so quietly that neither woman can even hear what she's said.

56

But it doesn't matter because Megumi, always impatient, is already back on the telephone, probably calling her brother or calling her sister again, making decisions, settling on the procedures they will all need to follow, and Kanae knows that her children will quickly take over her tragedy, they will push her farther than she wants to go.

After Jun's matches are finished, after they have eaten a quick lunch together at Jun's favorite restaurant, after they have driven back to Megumi's apartment and have started to say their good-byes, Megumi tells Kanae that they are all coming to Komachi the next day—Ken will come, but without his fiancée Etsuko, and Megumi will pick up Naomi on her way.

"I don't want Naomi to come alone. I'm not sure she can... otherwise I would come back with you right now."

They are saying good-bye and it is so easy, Kanae is thinking, this kind of good-bye, a smile, a wave, the assurance she will see them tomorrow; Kanae has wrapped Jun into her sweater like a cocoon and is dipping his head into the overgrown grass near the front door of the apartment and he is squealing with delight, he is fighting her embrace.

"Tell Grandpa I've been practicing. I can outrun him. I have supershoes."

Kanae settles him gently onto the lawn and unwraps him while a ladybug crawls onto his elbow and she leaves it, wondering if he'll notice the creature's tiny feet but he is already jumping up, skipping over to his mother.

"Are you okay in the house?" Megumi asks. "Do you want to stay here?"

Kanae shakes her head. "I'll get the house ready for all of you to stay tomorrow."

And she is getting into her car and waving good-bye, she is beeping her horn again and making a silly grin to her grandchild, like this is any other day of the week, any other day of her life, and as she drives off she feels a weight lifting off of her, just a breath of air, a lightness on the back of her neck—she has given herself a one-day reprieve.

霧島

The day ticks along, morning has passed on into afternoon, and now we are moving closer to evening and somewhere out over the ocean the winds have started pressing the storm toward us, we can feel it if we pay attention, a thickening in the air, a smell of heavy rain, and I am finished resting after my storytelling session, I am downstairs again and standing at the sliding glass door to the garden because she is here this evening, I am sure of it, and I am looking at the row of *sugi*, at the shadow and light that are fighting between each tree trunk because this is where she will sit when she comes, half-hidden in the tall grass and the bramble, her head straight and her ears pricked at attention. She's been coming for as long as I can remember, this same fox, her auburn face now nearly white, and if I am calm enough, if I am quiet, she will let me come near her, and if you were to enter my garden at this hour, you might be surprised at the sight of an old woman with her hand settled carefully atop the head of a fox.

You see, I healed her once a long time ago, healed her dislocated shoulder and sliced paw when I was only a girl and she was only a kit, and she is the only fox I have ever been able to heal, curious isn't it, although I have buried a few and I have courted a few who were injured. I have tried to tempt them into my garden with food, but they never came, they prefer their own healing or their own death, and so she is the only one who accepted my healing, and she visits from time to time, the only way she can repay her debt, because everyone knows that foxes are very serious about gratitude.

I'm waiting, I'm tensed, the light is moving across the grass and sliding toward the thicket of weeds I never bother to cut, and I'm afraid I will miss her—is that grass or the burnished gold of her coat?—so I open the door slowly, I take the risk, I step onto the porch and my whole body is tight with the thought that she's here and that once again she's come looking for me.

But the wind is changing too quickly, rushing through the trees and echoing through the chimes strung up against the house, and there I see it, the white tip of her tail as she turns on herself and slips deeper into the forest, her thin legs jumping over pine needles and off away to her den or another field, and I can do nothing but push my disappointment into the sleeve of my sweater and hold it tight against my body until it has no room to breathe and it dies, suffocated, against the hot evening air.

Kitsune. This half-god spirit. This messenger and cheat. So clever and so unattainable.

Poets must know all the stories, Grandfather would tell me, stopping me at his desk on my way between household chores or off to tea-making lessons, and slowly, over the years, he told me all of them, of all the animals, of all the monks and farmers, of clever women and selfish sisters, of sad young men and brave warriors, of the spirits living in the trees and in the water, of the spirits one must never cross, and I never really knew which were his own stories and which were older than anyone, stories that have always existed. And among all these stories it must be said that Grandfather had a love for foxes, or maybe it was me, and maybe there were stories I knew were meant for me and me alone, stories that no one else could know but him and me, and maybe Grandmother knew them too, but we were not to speak of them together.

Like the tale of the city man who helped a woman from a car on a dark night in summer, who helped her cross the street and into a restaurant, who joined her for a meal, who never again left her side—there was a marriage, there was a child, there were years of laughter—until one morning the woman grew ill, dangerously ill, and the man went to get a doctor even though she insisted he leave her to sleep it off, but he would not give her up so easily and when the doctor arrived, the bed was empty and the woman gone, and the only thing anyone ever saw was a fox racing through the front garden with a child's doll in its mouth.

Or the story of the farmer's child who lived in a ruin of a home, a sad and poor child, who adopted a fox from the forest, who brought it bread and sweet beans and let it eat from her hand, who followed it one day and slept the night in its den and was already growing a tail when her father found her and dragged her away and put up a fence to keep her inside and to keep the fox outside, because it would not do to let such boundaries grow thin.

And the last story, the only one of our secret stories that he ever wrote down, but with water on his brush and not ink, so although he'd written it, which meant that it was true, no one but me would know again how to trace out the *moji* on the paper, and this was about the little girl whose mother was believed to be a fox and luckily the girl had come out human although there was no telling what would happen to her later, to any of her children, so her family decided it was safer to keep their story a secret and the girl would become a woman who had never known a man's touch, who was forbidden to raise her eyes to the bright ones that sought her out, and she grew up to be as wise as a fox-child should be and this was supposed to be enough, said my grandfather, this was supposed to be a worthy and fair exchange.

Tonight it is easier to listen because the wind has kicked up, the air is moving more quickly through the sky and passing over the tops of people's heads, gathering up their words and their thoughts and carrying them around in its careful fast fingers, and so I turn away from the stand of trees, turn away from my longing for this *kitsune* and I sit down in the chair on the porch and let it all filter in. And I choose what I want because there is always too much, and tonight I am listening to the first contradictions, the first accusations, the half-spoken worries and gasps of surprise.

This evening we are learning the first hints of their story and the people of Komachi are wondering what it all might mean. Where has she gone? What is she doing? Where are the children? What is at stake? How must we think of her? So many stories starting up, so many possibilities—we are writing her and rewriting her, forgetting what we know of her character, forgetting our many conversations and the times we praised her, forgetting his devotion as well, and how often we have admired his mind and his thinking, and it is amazing how easily, how quickly really, a person can be turned inside-out and rewritten completely.

霧島

It is amazing how busy a body can be, like Kanae on this evening with her fingers to change the radio channel and her eyes flicking up and around to read road signs, and her nose smelling the smoke from a brushfire a few miles off the highway, her highway, this smooth lane of concrete providing her shelter in flight—such a safe little space, and she's buckled in and contained, constrained, a husk of metal and plastic around the seed of herself.

If she can just manage—and she is trying, she is trying so hard—to engage all five of her senses, then somehow she'll be fine, she'll have nothing to worry about, nothing to decide, all of her will be occupied and filled with purpose, and everything else will all fall into place like the road beneath the tread of her tires and the air that gets pressed and pushed to each side of her bumper as she rushes and races through this darkening night.

Just outside the first forests of the Fog Island Mountains her cell phone rings and it is not Alec, it is not one of her children, it is not the hospital, not one of her friends. She answers.

"I wondered if you could have dinner with me. I'm in Miyazaki for tonight, just one more evening."

Our Kanae is crying now, for the first time, but she rolls down her window and lets the noise of the passing cars mask her voice, and in this way she agrees, telling him she can be there in an hour and a half, driving fast along the blacktop twist of highway, up into the mountains again but passing the exit for Komachi and continuing on down the other side, heading for the other ocean this time, the enormous emptiness of the Pacific where it kisses the long strip of shoreline.

When she pulls into the parking lot where they have agreed to meet, Fumikaze is waiting for her outside his car even if it's raining, standing there on the concrete with his black umbrella a perfect frown over his neatly-cut hair and his shoes have been shined and his hand is so neat and steady on that umbrella handle and even his jacket looks new.

"I'm sorry I'm late," she says, "I was with my daughter in Kumamoto."
"It must be hard having your children so far away."

She nods to his compassion, closes her eyes. Has she loved them enough? Does she miss them now that they live away from home?

He drives her in his car to a restaurant on the north beach—Thai food—and he tells her it is supposed to be the newest thing, and she is humiliated for the trouble he is taking with her, but beneath her shame is the frightened beat of her pulse because she is not herself, she has shed something vital, a layer of her skin and the full current of her thought. Here now in this car, with this man, with this self that is no longer hers, she has achieved escape.

The restaurant is a trendy one, all soft cushion-covered benches and exotic fabrics, the scent of spices and hot oil, and there are so many young people, the women with their flashy handbags and slender toes, the waiters with their spiked hair and surfer boy slouches and then she realizes with a snap that what she's noticed has nothing to do with the atmosphere or the fashion but with the absence of a second look at her entrance—she has entered on the arm of a Japanese man and no one has noticed them, no one has made her aware of her couple.

He is thinking of buying an apartment in Miyazaki he tells her, and they are seated already, snacks before them on the table, and he was looking at property, he tells her, and then he is munching on a piece of dried squid and so she does it, she speaks with a voice that isn't really hers, she smiles and feigns interest.

"The city is becoming very expensive," she says.
"Is it difficult to live alone again?" he asks.

Kanae must blink now to bring him back into focus, to reverse his mistake, because he is the one who lives alone, this is what she should be asking of him, a chance to understand how to prepare herself, and the longer she waits to answer him, the deeper a flush of pink settles on his cheek bones and his nostrils flare just a little.

"I didn't mean . . . it was inconsiderate."

But Kanae is shaking her head, she is tasting her appetizer, watching her fork move from the plate to her mouth, quickly even, wondering how can she do this, how can she taste these spices and how can she be eating, how can she be sitting with this man at this table?

"Did you find something that you like?"

Fumikaze is fiddling with his food, hemming and hawing about his family and their criticism of his pending decision—why would he want to come back to Kyūshū? Why is he looking to the past? Nothing left for him there. What is he thinking?

"I remember your brothers enjoyed telling you what to do."
"I don't see them very often anymore. It's difficult . . . family."
"My daughter this morning . . . she is a single mother. She won't even tell me who the father is." Now it is Kanae's turn to look down at her plate, to fiddle with her chopsticks.
"My nieces tell me life is tough for women now, harder than when we were children, they say the lines of responsibility are all blurred, no one wants to take care of anyone anymore."
Her face growing hot, her stomach rebelling, she clenches her throat muscles. "Do you think this is true?"
"People need to establish strong connections, that is what's important."
"My other daughter is too shy to tell me anything, I don't know much about her life."
"That's what I should have done. I forgot about other people for too long."
"She might be terribly unhappy for all that I know . . ."
"I didn't ever forget about you."

It is strange, the feel of this man's fingers on her knuckles, the slide of his skin against her own, brushing the hollow between her first and second fingers, and she closes her eyes to let the feeling slip up her arm, opens her eyes, leaning forward now, looking at a vein pulsing on Fumikaze's smooth brow; she squeezes his hand in return just to feel the roll of his finger bones beneath her own and she watches him turn bashful, this gentle man, this ghost from her childhood, her youth.

Then she is standing, choking on the words, calling herself an idiot and telling him that she cannot only imagine this—has she said this out loud?—because pretending will not make this any easier and so she is reaching for Fumi's arm and saying that she'd like to leave, she is saying that she must finally practice. He is startled and fumbling with his wallet, throwing money on the table and together they are exiting the room, arm in arm, people will think of an emergency, two older people gripping each other's wrists and racing from a nice dinner—surely there was a phone call, someone, maybe one of their children has been hurt.

In the car she keeps a hold of his hand, she looks straight ahead, giving him directions to a love hotel on the outskirts of downtown and he only looks at her twice, he says nothing, and when they arrive they dash across the parking lot, they pay at the machine in the lobby and get their key, then they are sneaking along the hallway to their room.

Of course the room is in bad taste, all red velvet and animal prints, and the bed has curtains around it, the lights are pink and red, but this is an older hotel and only barely vulgar, what is important is that it's clean and that they do not speak, she couldn't bear to speak.

In the dimly lit bathroom they wash each other and Fumikaze is excited almost immediately, and here is Kanae holding his penis between her hands while he closes his eyes and he is reaching for her breasts and she waits for the moment when she'll feel his fingers but there is nothing, there is only the half-light and this object in her hands and the sound of his pleasure and then he is reaching between her legs and she surprises herself with the sound of a moan, with the push of her pelvis to get closer to him.

It is a surprise to find that she cannot get close enough to his body, and they are moving backward into the room, onto the bed, into each other and she hears nothing, feels only her skin against him, her mouth against his neck, the swollen friction of him moving inside her, but the minutes stretch out and then come together until one minute is bursting against another minute, and there is a second that feels like an hour, and he is panting against her even if the ache in her does not explode, it throbs as she waits for him to relax, she could move, just a centimeter and probably her body would release its tension but she holds herself rigid because none of this is for her, this sex with this man is too easy, too wonderful, too consuming, she will lose herself in it.

Upwelling

A curious thing has occurred—the sky over our island has heated up and even though the early night is spread now over the town and the last pink rays of the setting sun have vanished in the distance, even with this darkness the sidewalks are warm to the touch, the breeze, still only a breeze, brings only a sodden warmth, and even the windows, when we stand too close, offer little protection against the heat outside. Alec is standing with his forehead pressed against the big plate glass window in the upstairs common room of the hospital, his hands spread flat, his fingertips seeking the heat from the outside; he is like a fallen tree trunk, the smooth line of his body marking the angle from the floor to the window while the cool trickle of an air conditioner whispers against the skin of his neck, and the warm and the cold are battling within him as he seeks the heat and knows his body should just accept the cool embrace of the hospital's sterile air.

Behind him two teenagers are playing a game on a low table, swearing at each other in their sickness and subsequent freedom from parents and nighttime supervision, and one of the boys has a perfectly smooth and hairless skull and we all know he is far too young and Alec thinks again of that moment when he wondered whether he might not exchange his everywhere with Mr. Nishi, with this inadequate specimen of humanity—he scolds himself for the thought, but this is not a day for using up his inner hoard of mercy—but Alec knows there are no exchanges, there is no balance sheet somewhere and no great omniscient finger tallying up the number of fair deaths versus unfair deaths; he touches his body, hands pulled back from the warmth of the window and crossing over his chest, his fingers now pressing against his biceps, feeling the tendons roll under his touch and the healthy muscle resisting and he wonders if given the chance he would exchange, for this young man, for another worthy soul, for his own child, for Kanae . . . ah, here it is, such relief to suddenly glimpse this inner ladder of who-goes-where and where-am-I and yes, thank god, I have put someone above me, because it must be an ugly thing indeed to find oneself alone at the top of that list.

He isn't tired, even after today's surgery when they opened him up and looked around and determined what they had already suspected and so they closed him again, resealed his skin and stapled and pressed it together to hold his organs and blood inside, and the incision feels like a scratch now, it pulls a little, it tickles because his body is still misguidedly trying to heal in any way it can. They have told him to rest but he prefers walking, slowly, up and down the corridors of the different floors, into the common areas and around all these other people. He keeps waiting for someone to tell him he isn't allowed here, or here, or over here, especially when he walked through the children's wing, but no one even seemed to worry that he wasn't where he belonged; everyone is bowing to him, smiling at him.

And here at the nurses' station on his own floor, no one scolds him for his nightly ramble, these two women, one middle-aged and the other young, are deep in discussion, they don't even appear to notice he's arrived, and so he can't help it, he stands beside the desk because being unnoticed, passing unseen, is a feeling he's nearly forgotten about over all these years in our small town. Such a tall man, his shoulders stooped because this is how he has tried to make himself small to fit in and the women do not see him, and this is when he notices that one of the women is crying, the younger one, and her face is a wreck of worry and fear.

"But I can't stop visiting, it's my duty."
"If his parents say no . . ."
"They say I am putting pressure on him."
"Are they sure he is even aware? Has he shown any sign of improving?"

And here the young nurse trembles, her face becomes something else entirely, there is no thinking behind her features, only animal emotion, only lack of control, and it is bad timing because right at this second the older nurse has noticed Alec's presence and now they are both staring at him, and the younger nurse must duck her head and turn away, but it is too late, Alec is reaching forward with a hand and a few careless words come tumbling out of him, "Are you okay? What is wrong?"

But everyone can see she is not okay, and the older nurse frowns at him, because what business is it of his, why can't he pretend he hasn't seen . . . but she is quickly refashioning her face into its professional mask and asking what he needs and standing and walking toward him and before he even realizes it, she is leading him back to his room, she has a hand on his arm, like a mother would, a broad palm steady on his forearm, her fingers blunt and firm. The only sound is the slap of her working slippers on the empty linoleum and the hum of a fluorescent light bulb about to flicker and go out, and the nurse eyeballs it while they walk and Alec lowers his head even further because he has got a glimpse of something he understands all too easily. No one needs to guess at Nurse Noriko's situation—even Alec will learn the details when two nurses stop to talk outside his room later this evening when most people assume he is asleep.

A motorcycle, a slick patch of pavement, a young man not wearing a helmet. Young Nurse Noriko's boyfriend is in another hospital, in another town further south on our island, his body intubated and still covered in bruises, for the moment the machines are keeping him alive.

"Is Mr. Chester comfortable?"

They have reached his room and the last thing Alec wants to do is go inside, no matter what time it is, no matter what schedule of treatments and discussions they have planned for him tomorrow, and so he thanks this kindly nurse and only pretends to go through the door, because she can't make him go in there, she can't make him face that single hospital bed and that limp magazine lying half-open on the extra chair, so he waits until she walks away and then he's off again, this time toward the main entrance of the hospital, which is quiet at this time of night, there are only a handful of people sitting in those stiff-backed plastic chairs, and the night receptionist is reading on an iPad and the lights from the computer have made the lenses of her eyeglasses glow green.

He could walk outside right now, he could, even wearing this bathrobe and these slippers, and maybe he'll do it, watch him, he is hovering near those sliding automatic doors, he is practically dancing on his tiptoes, this tall man, this gentle giant of an English teacher who has loved us all so much, been more than kind to our difficult children and been so patient with our unworthy tongues—no, he won't go out just yet, this is still too soon.

"Alec?"

His head is down. He won't answer his friend. Shingo Ishikawa. "Alec, listen..."

Alec is turning now, head up, arms at his sides, those claws have fallen from his fingers, the tension is falling from his shoulders, this is Alec giving up his anger and his restlessness because here is a friend asking him to keep control and Alec has always been ready to answer to this kind of request.

Side by side now, looking out the window, looking past their reflections, one short and white-coated, one tall and gray-haired, looking over the few shadow hulls of car in the parking lot and further onward toward the mountains, toward that black line of ridge and the almost purple sky that sets it alight behind our Komachi.

"I've got a chess board in my office..."

Alec smiles, of course Shingo has a chess board in his office, this is how his friend has managed to beat him all these years, all those times when an English lesson turned into a chess match, each man struggling over the words at first, but in most recent years, each man talking swiftly to the other—in English, in Japanese.

So off they go, one short man, one tall man slumping only a little now, and they will spend the next few hours moving those chess pieces around and not talking, for the first time, their game will not be played to the backdrop of an easy conversation, to questions of translation and expression, they will silently move their chess pieces around and Shingo will take comfort in the fact that he is helping his friend keep busy through these awful hours, and Alec will move each pawn, each knight, his bishops several times, and he will be wondering, with each gentle pick and settle of Shingo's heavy chess pieces on the wooden board, *Is this all? Oh, my God, this is all.*

霧島

Here with Kanae, we are closer to the sea where the wind is picking up, where the rain has finally started to fall, she can hear it pinging—gently for now—on the thin roof of the love hotel, and she is lying straight as a board while beside her Fumikaze is curled into himself, facing her, sleeping such a silent sleep; he hardly makes a sound as the air enters and exits his body, and she is frowning in the dark because there should be no peace allowed around her, no stillness like his tender repose admitted into this room.

So she is sliding herself out of the bed, she has never been so quiet, she is crossing this tiny cubicle of a room with its garish colors and questionable fabrics and she begins searching the floor line, eyes roaming over the piles of clothing, the little humps of their discarded slippers, tracing along the blurred outlines of the objects and chair legs, until . . . there it is, her purse, and she tiptoes over to it, rummaging inside while sliding across the carpet into the bathroom, and it doesn't take her long to find what she is looking for; she has her hand around the tiny sewing scissors and she closes the door behind her, gently now, not even a tell-tale click, and now the light is on and it takes her a long moment but eventually she is able to raise her head and look herself in the eye.

She forces herself to stare, scissors wrapped in the fleshfold of her hand, and there is not a sound from the outer room, not a sniffle, not a sigh—and what a surprise it is to discover Fumikaze's untroubled sleep, she had imagined him a restless man, she had envisioned insomnia, even drinking or chain-smoking, some vice cultivated in the valley of his loneliness, some reason for her to feel sorry for him, but there is truly none and she can only stare at this reflection in the mirror. This sixty-something woman with those gray-brown eyes and slender nose, those lines like folded tissue paper at her eyes—and now her eyebrows are raised in surprise, are asking this woman in the mirror to stop playing her game, to get over herself, to take a real inventory of her person, because her face is giving nothing away.

"You have opened your hands and dropped it all," she whispers to herself in English, wanting to put something between herself and the silent sleeper, but this change in language isn't enough, she wants different words, only words that she herself could understand, made-up words that could become a physical apology, something she could pick up again and carry with her into Alec's hospital room, an object she could place in his hands and all would be erased.

Remember the three sorries, they used to tell their children, and the children would stare back at them, faces sometimes still twisted in anger or broken with sorrow, bodies tense and curved, but they were easy children and they would wait and listen to be reminded about saying sorry, feeling sorry, and the third and most important sorry of all, showing sorry. And so Kanae is counting now, on her fingers, in the thick yellow light of this bathroom, counting off each sorry with a little huff, hoping that in repetition she will make them come true.

Oh, we hear it now, the rain is coming down outside and these rowdy drumbeats get her up off the edge of the bathtub and climbing inside of it, pushing back the sliding window so the burst of hot air strikes her face, blows her hair off her shoulders, but this isn't enough so she pushes back the metal screens, pushing hard because they stick and then it's on her, the hard rain, the early lashing of the coming storm and she closes her eyes and this is helping, this is taking her out of herself. And so she lets it beat against her, wondering for a moment if the noise might wake Fumikaze but, no, it can't, it won't, not tonight, not when she needs this violence for herself and sharing it would only make it all so hollow.

"You have opened your hands and dropped it all."

Has she said this? Nothing is less certain because she is nothing but a statue now, frozen with her mouth a little open and her eyes closed tight, and maybe she isn't even with us anymore, not for now, she has let enough of herself slip out through the window that she is now nearly as peaceful as that sleeping body in the other room.

Just a short distance from our statue is the ocean and its surface is a froth of movement, all those waves made by the winds, the same winds that are bringing up the denser, cooler water from the depths, churning our Pacific and making it something else entirely as the storm grows. No longer gathering, this storm is actually upon us, already driving along the beaches and moving across the edge of the island, ready to hedge its way inland, and there—hear it?—the first of the thunder. We haven't even noticed the lightning, but now Kanae's eyes are open and she is moving and she has purpose and we can only watch her again.

The scissors are still inside her closed fist and she brings them up into the light; they are small and dull but they will do, and so she is facing that mirror-woman again and pulling up a lock of hair, it only takes a snip, a heavy pressure from her fingers to cut through these hairs. Snip. Again. Snip. Again. Around and around her salt-and pepper head, not caring about the length except that it all must go, and the scissors flash with a bolt of lightning and the hands tremble as the crack of thunder splits the sky. But she is still cutting and turning her head and reaching backward for those hard-to-reach pieces, and eventually—how long did it take her? Maybe twenty minutes?—it is all gone. Just a cap remains, curling toward her head with the damp of this night.

The memory is painful but she lets it come and she lets it sit beside her in this tiny space, and she can feel his hands again on her neck and ears, a steadying balance on her shoulder as he took the scissors and did as she'd requested . . . because they were young, not long married, no children yet, and they would take their baths together in the evenings, spend hours in a half-light nakedness and it seemed impossible there could be so much pleasure from only two bodies, two finite volumes of skin on skin. And he used to cut her hair back then, because she kept it simple—long and straight, it was the fashion—so he would comb out her damp hair and place the blade of the scissors against her naked back and trim as straight a line as he could.

She nicks an earlobe, not on purpose, only her fingers have begun to shake, despite the warmth outside, our Kanae is cold, there are goose bumps along her arms and up to her now-naked neck, so she tosses the scissors into the trash and closes the window now, sliding gently, muting the storm outside. Then she sweeps the hair as best she can, scraping with her fingers along the edges of the sink and rinsing it all away and in the same movement she dries her hands and turns off the light, purse over her shoulder, and now she is back in the other room, standing over this sleeping form, this peaceful gentle man, who has no idea what she has done and that she is about to leave this room, is about to take his car and leave him stranded in this dingy place in order to get back to her own, to get back to herself and to our little town, to make herself do what she should have been able to do when our story began so many days ago.

霧島

We are not many people but the neighborhood is joined together tonight, we are placing sandbags along the riverbank, protecting the old *onsen* from the water that will surely come, the flooding can be strong along this little stream when the great rivers up higher in the mountains swell and overflow, and so I am here to help as well, I have brought a tall thermos of tea down for the young men who are carrying such heavy loads, and for the women who are helping too, there is Old Hoshi pretending to carry sand, there is his daughter following him, wishing he would go back inside, you will get sick in this weather, she is telling him, you are shaming me, is what she doesn't dare to say.

The rain is heavy and the trees whipping their thin branches through the air, and so those who are not working at the edges of the stream, those who are not bagging sand out of the back of a truck, are huddled up here under the eaves of the *onsen* building, on this small veranda with its slender benches and lonely vending machine, we are just a handful of women and some teenagers, those not quite old enough to help in the dark and the rain, but old enough to still be awake, we are standing out here in the darkness, and we are passing along what we've heard so far about the typhoon and if it has damaged our little town.

"The road out to the high school is impossible already."
"I heard that Kawakami's farm lost an outbuilding."
"Some tourists are stranded at the *yakiniku* restaurant–aren't they lucky?"
"I heard the hospital had to put in another generator."

And here it begins again, this mention of the hospital brings everyone to attention, because you must remember, this is Kanae Endo's childhood neighborhood, she grew up just two houses from the *onsen*, when there were only a handful of old homes on this road on the outskirts of Komachi, and we have all known her since she was little, we have followed her life some, her marriage to a foreigner being an event to remember, her keeping that foreigner in our town instead of disappearing after him like so many other women, no, Kanae somehow managed to make him one of us, and then, of course, Alec has been such a perfect foreigner—he has never surprised us in the wrong way.

"Have you heard what they are saying?"
"It's terrible, the poor man."
"Does anyone know what he has?"
"Has anyone seen her?"

The teenage girl's eyes are open wide, the tops of her high cheek-bones glowing in the damp and the moonlight and she wants to know what we're talking about, she is whispering to her granny, Misako Ishimura, she is asking what is this all about, and her granny is whispering back to her, and now I must really interrupt, even if I have been standing in the shadows and some of these people will have forgotten that I am really here.

"Are we really sure she hasn't been to the hospital?"
There are nods and chatter.
"But I mean have you seen Chester-Sensei? Have you asked him about it?"
"What are you getting at, Azami?" There is a pitch of high laughter; Misako has always had a horrible witchy laugh. Then she half-whispers, "Anyway, surely you should know, Azami, you old fox!"
The teenagers look at me again and now I must smile at them as Misako giggles and makes her silly allusions, I must smile at them as I have been smiling at the children since I became old enough to frighten them—before, when we were all just children, I was the one who was frightened and would have to run away.

There is a boom of thunder overhead and one of the tree limbs shakes itself free from the tree and drops to the ground, startling Old Hoshi finally once and for all even if it missed him by several meters, and he makes his way up to the porch and collapses onto the bench in his dirty wet clothes, his sleeves are rolled up to his elbows and his pant legs rolled up to the knee, his ropey little calves flex as he bounces his legs, twitching a little, wanting a drink no doubt, and I offer him a cup of warm tea and he thanks me, not seeing me.

"But you remember, Hoshihara, certainly you know all about it . . ."
He is squinting up at Misako, his mouth open as if this will make him hear her better.
"You went to school with Azami, wasn't it silly how she was teased?"
He looks at me now, wiping the water from his forehead with the back of his hand and drinking the tea in one gulp.

"Oh, we were silly children, of course," Misako is saying, mostly to her granddaughter but loud enough for everyone to hear. "Children are naturally cruel, and there were so many stories back then, you young people know nothing of our folktales, but anyway..."

She is prattling now, speaking too much, the teenagers have turned their bodies away from her, the young mother is only half-listening while she changes her baby's diaper, looking over our heads to check on her husband off with the other workers, and I am still smiling, ready to laugh if I must, ready to be sillier than Misako can even imagine, but Old Hoshi is still staring at me and I feel my skin crawling now, I feel that urge to find the nearest tree and climb up into it as high as I can go, but he is only asking for another cup of tea and waving his hand at Misako for quiet, pretending to some male authority he no longer has, and so I pour him another but he reaches for my wrist so quickly I don't have time to pull away, and then he is holding tight and whispering up at me.

"You've turned out all right, but you've kept your place."
Before I can stop myself I have turned my hand around and let my fingernails grip his skin, I am holding on as sharply as I can and Old Hoshi has started to laugh, he is leaning his head back and shaking his hand free, laughing and shouting now, "Well, you still have a vixen's bite."

I roll my eyes because this is an old drunk, and everyone knows it, and whatever he has said he has only said to me, and it doesn't matter anymore because I have moved quickly to the other side of the veranda, I am pouring tea for two young men who have come up to take a break, and behind me Misako is still laughing her silly laugh but she is no longer telling the children about my grandmother's superstitions, she is talking about the television and her favorite variety show, about her favorite old pop singer, and how she's sent in her money to win tickets to see him, to be a part of the audience, and luckily just then the storm surges above us, it's a kind of mercy, it silences her and then we are all staring out into the darkness and watching the men crouched over the edge of the stream, watching them slip a little in their haste, watching them continue to pile the sandbags and we are hoping now, hoping that it will be enough because this storm is about to show us what it's worth.

霧島

Here we are on the morning of the third day, if Alec were at home he would be preparing for a lesson with Mr. Nagakutsu, drinking tea perhaps, staring out the window of his study into the garden, at the way the wind would be pushing at the rows of flowers and how each gale might rip another handful of petals from their bases and lash them against the leaves of another tree to make it appear that the leaves were bleeding, and he'd get up and find Kanae, wake her even, and make her come to the window and show her this moment of beauty from the storm.

Instead, Alec is slipping out of his hospital bed and moving into the hallway, it is early enough that the night nurses are still on duty, just finishing up their reports and tidying the desk and getting their patient reports ready for handover to the day staff, and so he glides past them and at the bend in the corridor he bows good morning to a very old woman shuffling near the fire doors, he is looking right and left, the woman's back is to him, no one else is coming from either direction and so he opens a door and enters an old, unused X-ray room where sometime in the middle of the night, just before going to sleep, he stashed his street clothing in one of the empty cupboards. Just to be sure, Alec pushes a chair up against the door and then he is slipping out of his hospital trousers and t-shirt and into his slacks and button down, and he is wriggling his toes in his hiking sandals, which feel so stiff and rough against the bottom of his feet after these days of wearing slippers and going barefoot.

A noise. People have stopped just outside the doorway, and judging from their voices it is a young couple—oh, Alec knows these sounds, the woman is giggling and the man has made some compliment about her eyes which makes Alec smile, because it is always the eyes, compliment a woman's eyes and she will think you have complimented her character, her soul.

"You'll save me from the trauma of the day," this young man is saying, a touch of poetry in his inflection. "Your face is alive, it changes everything."

"But I can't have lunch with you today, I have to help Tsuruta Sensei with paperwork."

The young man's silence is sharp and immediate and Alec waits for the woman to enter it, to try to shuffle it away, but she doesn't and Alec is intrigued, even today, and so he closes his eyes and wonders at this couple and who they might be and whether their story is an interesting one.

The young man speaks first. "His patients aren't serious cases, he doesn't need you to cheer him up."

Laughter, then a coy response, "What time are you off tonight?"

Before Alec realizes it, the couple has moved along and he is alone again in his hiding spot, shivering a little but not from the cold because this room is hotter than the rest, its air conditioner turned off, but Alec wipes the sweat from his forehead with a clammy finger and rests a moment against the door. Just the exertion needed for this secrecy has made him tired. And so he leaves his flimsy hospital garments in a wadded ball in the trash can, slips back into the hallway, and takes the stairs down to the front entrance, this is his biggest gamble, he will not go completely unnoticed, someone will remember him leaving this morning, he just hopes that by then he will be far enough away.

"Chester Sensei," nods a sleepy taxi driver.

"*Ohayō gozaimasu*," he responds with his own quick nod, still walking. Good Morning. Not an honest statement.

It is time to take stock—the small incision in his side aches, but only a little, his head is feeling tender, his hands are trembling, his stomach is wondering vaguely about some food, and he knows the painkillers he swallowed after his chess game with Shingo will only last for a few more hours, and he will be on his own again, just as he was last week, with this everything. How bad can it be?

Alec stops quickly at the local Family Mart to buy some potato salad, a sandwich and a bottle of ice cold green tea, but over near the magazine rack there are two housewives discussing the cancer-fighting properties of green tea and Alec nearly laughs in their faces, nearly falls against them in his sudden mirth, but he keeps himself tucked over, tightly pulled in, he is nearly invisible, and in a few minutes he is out the door again and walking back toward his home.

It takes him nearly forty minutes to reach his neighborhood on foot, and when he arrives he does not stand for a second at the half-empty driveway, he knew she would not be here, and he is no longer angry—he is baffled, worried, frustrated, and he only hopes she is spending her nights with one of their children—but his feet move a little more quickly, his breathing chuffs just a second longer, he is exhausted, there is sweat pouring down his back and the pain, a throb really, has begun to beat again within him. The cancer is his heart.

He packs almost nothing, a change of underwear, socks and shirts, some books and a stack of crossword puzzles, and then he wonders about leaving a note but what would he say, who would he say it to? He isn't even sure what it is exactly he's doing right now, he is refusing the hospital and he is refusing his home, he is craving motion, but before he leaves he pulls down the ladder to the attic and scrambles up, finds the box marked Megumi and opens it to rifle through the drawings she made when she was child but this makes him smile because really, his Meg was never very much of a child in the first place, and now he is not smiling anymore because he knows which drawing he wants, the one of their house, a wobbly sketch in charcoal done when she was a teenager, done the year one of the volcanoes in Hawaii had erupted and they'd all seen too many images on TV of hot lava pouring down the hillsides, destroying houses.

"Japan is a volcano," she'd said to him. "*Kirishima Renzan wa kazan bakari desu.*" The Fog Island Mountains are nothing but volcanoes.

"These are different. They are old. Dormant." He explained this meant they were sleeping, that they burped from time to time but they weren't ever going to erupt.

So he is folding this childish picture into the top of his small bag and heading back downstairs, he is refusing a tour of the building and he knows that the memory of this house will clutch at him in the next few days, he is sure of this, and he is also vaguely ashamed to be feeling so emotional about a structure—this is only a house, only a house, only a house. And then he is closing the door behind him and getting into his car.

It comes to him in the driver's seat, hands on the steering wheel, a selfish wish, he is thinking that if he could do it all again, he would get sick much much earlier, when his children were all small, and then he could gather them up into his arms, all three of them against his own chest, all within his long arms and he could feel each of their small bodies against his own, their heartbeats thumping wildly in the intimacy of this crushed embrace and he could say good-bye, all at the same time, all that is important to him, because he knows that as adults, everything is all wrong, he can't stand the idea of dealing with each of them, each different reaction, each wayward emotion, he will have to look them in the eye and see what they understand about him and what his leaving means to them.

As they folded up the chess table the night before, Shingo mentioned all the ways there are to help make Alec comfortable and he also offered to call Alec's children—neither man mentioned Kanae, and to get through this moment, to get past it as quickly as possible, Alec turned and thanked his friend, and when Shingo asked why, Alec said, "For telling me . . . I know it isn't always customary."

There was a pause and suddenly these two were no longer in this hospital, they were discussing a notion of Japanese culture like so many others they had discussed; here was their friendship, waiting for them both, all over again.

"Sometimes knowing will make things worse, for the family, for everyone . . . but you . . . you have always been different."

Even in his death he will be a foreigner, somehow this comes as a comfort to Alec.

霧島

Her children are assembled in the driveway, looking at her, looking at her shortened hair, but none of them say a word, they do not dare ask her what she's done, why she's done it, even if Naomi's forehead wrinkles with a frown—they must think her so old fashioned, they must think she is already resigned.

"Where's Jun?"
"I left him with Mrs. Kenta, I have to be back tonight."
Then a flutter at her wrist, Naomi's quiet face. "But I'm staying here, Mother, I had some vacation coming to me anyway."
"You don't have to do that." This a reflex, said much too quickly because Kanae already knows that she cannot change what is already happening, she cannot stop the movement of her children as they

circle around her in protection.

Naomi dips her head. "I wanted to . . ."

Kanae sees that her youngest daughter will not make it through this, she will break like glass, and there will be pieces of her strewn about Kanae's life.

Ken'ichi is already coming down the steps, he's locked the door behind him, he walks so much like his father. "I have to get back tomorrow, but will come again in a few days—"

"Can we get going already?" This from Megumi, already she is rigid with irritation, her body pulled away from her siblings, away from her mother, tense and taut and ready to explode.

All of her children move now into her little car, and no one asks her where she would like to sit, but Ken'ichi is driving and she has been placed into the backseat with Naomi, like a child, and she resents it, she is not this kind of sixty-something, she is not ready for Alec's illness to make her this old, to make it that she must be chauffeured around like a grandmother.

The words are out before she can stop them, she can only manage to reduce them to a whisper, "What a grandmother you make me."

"And about to be made one again," says Megumi, nudging her brother, "Tell her, Ken."

Ken turns his head to the car and is silent for a moment, the smooth arc of his hands at ten and two o'clock, and Kanae can tell he would like to snap at his sister, bark her into a corner, but he keeps it inside, he says only to Kanae, gently, "We wanted to tell you together. Etsu is expecting."

"But you're not married yet." This isn't what she means to say but it is what her brain does to what she'd really wanted to say, something about the future and housing and their jobs.

Megumi is chuckling, "Need we remind you how things work?"

But Ken is shushing his sister now, looking more like an older brother than the family's youngest, and he glances at Kanae in the rearview, and Naomi is hedging a hand in her direction, like she might need comforting, and Kanae can only shake her head at her children, and wonder how they can think of her as old and easily shockable. Her children will never imagine what she knows, what her body had done in the past twenty-four hours.

"I'm sorry, Ken'ichi, congratulations. Is Etsu feeling well?"
Ken nods. This isn't the time.

Naomi has withdrawn her hand and is fanning herself quietly, Kanae reaches toward her now, more comfortable in this role, and places a hand on her knee—as a child, Naomi wore this same frightened expression whenever she was asked to do something new, she has never seemed to have grown out of her fear of change, and Kanae realizes that Naomi, of all her children, is more familiar with betrayal than anyone else, this world that is changing on her and renewing itself all the time, new technologies and products, people who do the unexpected, ask her to accept what she would never do herself.

"Does Ishikawa Sensei know we're coming?"
"Of course."
"Does Father know we're all coming this morning?"
Kanae watches out the window and fingers the bare skin of her neck, "I expect he does."

What no one expects is to learn that Alec has vanished, and no amount of guessing and arguing will tell them where he is—Nurse Uchida believes he must have left during the shift change, and Shingo Ishikawa wonders if he might have left after their late chess match, and young Nurse Noriko worries that he's gotten lost in the hospital somewhere.

"What did he say last night?"
"Nothing. No one said anything."

"But his surgery? What were the results?"

The doctor is quiet, frowning. "We discussed his surgery before supper. We did not discuss it again."

"Mother, how was he last night?"

"But we spoke again in the evening. Just he and I. We discussed his options."

Kanae is not looking at her children. She is looking at the yellow curtains someone has hung up on the window. She is looking at the sky beyond the window and she is thinking, wondering, how the storm has managed to maintain its intensity for so many hours now.

Shingo Ishikawa is firm. "He took the news very well."

"You told him? Everything?"

The gray-haired doctor nods. Inside the right sleeve of his jacket he is using his thumb nail to pick at a hangnail on his ring finger. "I told him everything. This is all my fault."

And then Naomi is crumbling, putting a hand across her face, hiding herself away in shame at the strength of her emotions, and Megumi sits down in the chair by the wall, but then she gets up and moves to lean against the bed that Alec slept in, and she looks ready to rip the sheets from it, or stomp on the pillows, and the only person quiet enough to go on is Ken'ichi and he is asking several questions of Nurse Uchida and reaching for his mother with a hand.

Nurse Uchida is perplexed, "He didn't seem that upset. Not so much to . . ."

Megumi is already pulling her cell phone from her purse, already calling the police.

"Yes," says Ishikawa, "It is a horrible possibility."

Everyone is looking at Kanae and Kanae is watching her younger daughter crying, so she reaches for her daughter but the gesture is empty because Kanae knows that Alec has not snuck out of the hospital to go kill himself quietly somewhere else, this is not a decision he would make, they aren't considering him properly, they are behaving as if they don't know him at all, and she wants to shout at them.

"No," she says, "He is angry."

"Of course he is, that's normal."

"But this is not your fault, Shingo, he is angry with me."

This is when Megumi, her face tilted away from her cell phone, sweeps over her mother with a long arm, telling her to stop being so silly, to stop being irrational, but Kanae cuts her short with a snap, and it feels good for once to stop Megumi's anger so quickly, to cut it off with a decisive movement, she has always allowed her oldest daughter too much freedom in this anger of hers, because she was embarrassed by it, but she sees now that she was wrong, Megumi is just an angry person and there is nothing she will ever do that will change that.

"This has nothing to do with you, Megumi. This is me. Your father and me. He's dying."

"Kanae, please . . . sit down, take a moment to calm yourself. This is troubling news."

She waves the doctor away, "He's dying, do you hear me?"

She does not sit down, in fact she begins to back herself out of the room, out of this little box where she left Alec on his own, and if she raises her arm to her nose she is sure she can smell Fumikaze's cologne, somewhere on her skin his cologne has soaked in, and so she leaves the room, finds her telephone in her purse and dials Alec's number, because he is alive, she is sure he is alive. But there is no answer and she must put her phone away, and here is her son Ken'ichi beside her, whispering, urging her to talk to the police. She is looking at him and she sees that he is a man, he is about to become a father, and over near Alec's bed Megumi is comforting Naomi and she remembers that Megumi has never turned her anger on her younger fragile sister, and this gives her hope, and so when Ken'ichi bows to her, when his eyes come up and he says, Okāsan, she nods her head, because this is what she will remember later, not the hours pacing at home, not the detailed discussions with the police, not the argument she will pick with Megumi in a short while, but this moment, her son's patience, the ghost of Alec on his face, his *please*.

Feeder Bands

You think you know a person, thinks Shingo Ishikawa, you think you understand them and how they think and what they want, and he is puzzled by this, still now, after so many years of doctoring in our small town, so many families and their illnesses have passed through his hands, and he has healed them or occasionally not healed them, and sometimes he is surprised by a patient's thinking or wishes or words, but most often, what his doctoring has taught him is that nothing can really be expected because, when it is all finished and the cells are multiplying in all the wrong ways, we are mysteries to ourselves.

It is late morning now and he is not on duty, he was supposed to go home last night and today would be his day off, a day to drive into Miyazaki and visit his brother maybe, if the roads remain drivable, or go to a movie in the early evening when the theater will be mostly empty, or maybe just watching baseball or soccer on the television, another of his favorite things to do, but he is sitting at his desk instead, still in the same clothes he wore last night and fumbling with some paperwork, chewing on the edges of his fingernails and pushing the sharp edges of his teeth against those soft nail beds and knowing that in a moment he will get up and leave this office and offer himself to help in any way he can, to look for Alec or Alec's body. But for just this frozen second Shingo is remembering a winter afternoon and a teacher's hospital in another city, the feel of the clipboard in his young hands, and the sturdy shape of the senior doctor at his side and they are both watching Kyōsuke Inomura in his hospital bed.

"You don't have to tell me, Doctor."
"There is nothing to tell. You must relax."
"It doesn't really hurt, I know what that means."
"You'll be just fine tomorrow."

And they stand there—Shingo listening, watching, learning—while Kyōsuke Inomura closes his eyes. His breathing is labored and the minutes pass and no one moves, and once he is fully asleep Inomura begins to shout, his body convulsing, but there are nurses to hold his arms and the senior doctor stands quietly, he makes no sign to Shingo, he makes no comment, and before anyone can look at their watches, before anyone can discuss the details of this man's advanced illness, Kyōsuke Inomura finally stops moving, he leans his head back and opens his mouth and the sound of the last air coming out of his throat is like wind tearing through a broken pipe, and then he is still. Too still. And Shingo must bow quickly and leave the room because although he has practiced surgery on other bodies, although he has spent hours with the deceased, learning to unfold them, learning from their preserved organs, this is the first time he witnesses the crossover and although it is a selfish thing, he knows this, he has always known this, he was not watching old man Inomura, he was reaching inside his own chest and testing the strength of his heartbeat and building up the walls around his eyes that would make it possible for him to witness these deaths, year after year, again and again, and he would not see the person anymore, he would only know his own *beat, beat, beat* and feel safe in its strength.

"Alec, it will not be painful, I will promise you this." Said at the end of their chess game last night, said carefully between two friends of understanding, two mature men who can speak of these fragile things.

But Alec did not answer him, Alec only shook his head and flashed his hand across the air between them, like wiping something clean, and this is what is bothering our gentle Dr. Ishikawa, this is what he cannot figure out, that Alec's face lost its fear, and so he is standing now, removing his doctor's white coat and putting on his favorite baseball cap, for the wind outside is growing fiercer, the hospital lights have flickered once already, and out in the hallway the nurses are gathering at the station, getting ready for a hospital-wide meeting that will list the tasks they must accomplish before the typhoon arrives above us.

"Ishikawa-Sensei, please ... "

The police have questions, this is only natural, they are holding out a photograph of Alec, and Shingo is nodding, yes, of course, this is him, yes, that's his grandson in his arms, it looks a few years old, but Alec hasn't changed, he is maybe a little thinner...

"He will be easy to identify, he's a very tall foreigner. Everyone knows him and he's ... well, he's my friend." Words broken off in his throat.

The police man has nodded severely and is turning away in kindness and Shingo is wiping at his eyes, and the nurses are giving him their backs, pretending not to see him, they are a courteous group of women, and he is groping for a chair and leaning over against his hands, rubbing the shock away, reaching for the certainty of this friendship, surely Alec would not do such a thing, and then one of the nurses breaks rank with the others, she is coming to him, sitting beside him and putting a hand on his shoulder and he can only look at this hand and shake his head, and then he is nodding again, he is standing, he is bowing to them all and thanking them for their hard work, and then he is walking quickly to the doorway and the gusts of wind and calling out to the policeman and asking them where he is to go, where can he help?

霧島

Old Hoshi crouches to the ground—it must be around here somewhere, he is thinking, and then he's crawling on his hands and knees, his back already soaked through with rain, the edges of his jacket trailing along in the mud, and he has to push them out of the way as he searches the dirt for the latch to the hidden door. *Where is it? Where is it?* Old Hoshi is getting impatient now, his heart beating quickly and his tongue already dry in his mouth, even if he's promised himself he won't touch a drop of it when he finds it, he just wants to move it, make sure it's safe from the storm. His hand catches on something, no, just a tree root, wait, that's right, here it is, and he's sweeping his old hand once more and catching his fingers in the rope loop that pulls up the wooden hatch-door and now he's looking down into the old storm cellar and he's smiling because the rest of his family has forgotten about this place, it isn't a good cellar really, too close to the river and fills with water at the base, but a perfect place for keeping his *shōchū*, except in a storm, and so he's going down the stone steps and he's got his flashlight and it's glinting across the gold lettering of the cartons.

But he hasn't planned very well, has he? Because how is he going to get these cartons back to his little room at the *onsen*, how will he carry them up the road without a crate or a bag, and this kind of problem is exactly what will get him to break his promise this afternoon, because he's starting to get a little cold out here in the wind and the rain, he's starting to feel pretty sorry for himself, what with his good ideas now gone bad, and so Hoshi is pacing a little, up and down the steps of the cellar, taking a sip then taking a gulp from one of the cartons, walking over to the road to look at the distance from this former outbuilding with its forgotten about cellar to the *onsen*, then another drink, sitting down for a moment and letting the *shōchū* warm him up, walking back over to the road, and then he sees a car flash past and then another one, and so he's grinning again, he can't be beat so quickly, he just needs a bag or a box and surely...

Yes, surely someone will stop for him, and once he's got his cartons—six of them, what a treasure—of this delicious Aka Kirishima into a rough canvas bag found on another shelf in the shelter, he's back out onto the road, now he's just an old man stuck in the rain, waving his arm at the passing cars and hoping someone will give him a lift back up to his house and of course one of the cars stops for him, pulling right up against the edge of the road and Old Hoshi is happy to slide right in and put his cartons at his feet, only what a surprise it is to see the driver isn't Japanese, and Hoshi almost turns to get out again, but the driver is bowing and greeting him with perfect politeness and he even knows his name and so Hoshi takes another look and something about this foreign man looks familiar, so he must be okay, and Hoshi relaxes again into his seat.

"It's unlucky to get caught out in this weather, Hoshihara-san, can I take you back up home or are you going to town?"

"Thank you for your trouble, I'm just going home. Just up the road. It isn't far."

"Yes, I know. Are you all right? You've gotten very wet."

But Old Hoshi is giggling, he's warm from the belly on out, he's got his *shōchū* safe and he'll probably even be able to get it past his pesky daughter and her constant scolding because she's too worried about the basement flooding and about one of the old trees falling onto the roof and the wind breaking one of the upstairs windows of the bathhouse, and so he tells his driver that it's a perfect day, no one needs to worry about the weather and when he peeks at the white man, he starts to feel a little funny because this gray-haired Westerner isn't smiling very much.

"Say, don't look so down, sir, it's just a little rain, isn't it? We're a tough little island, we've weathered worse."

And the man is nodding at him, not smiling, but nodding, and Hoshi is feeling brave from all the fire in his belly, feeling happy now that he's out of the muck and the rain, and so he's getting chatty, and he asks his driver what he's got to be so unhappy about, and the driver looks at him and just shakes his head, smiling a little now.

"It's nothing for you to worry about Hoshihara, here we are, and there's your daughter coming to meet us, so I'm going to let you out just here, you don't mind walking the last bit."
"What's the rush, Gaijin-san, can't you take an old man to the door?"
"I'm sorry I can't. Thank you for understanding."

And Old Hoshi is scrabbling out of his seat, clutching his bag and grumbling a bit because this hasn't worked out how he expected, now he's got his daughter coming who will ask too many questions and this foreigner is bowing to him, that grim smile only a stretch of the lips, and Hoshi can't stop himself now, the heat in his belly has turned to irritation and he's grabbing a hold of the white man's arm and he's telling him to watch his ways, he's saying, I've got an eye on you, and he's saying, I'm careful about foreigners, okay, never can be too careful, and a little bit of spit is flicking out when he speaks, but the foreigner just shakes his arm away and is nodding politely and the car is driving away, the man hunched at the wheel, and Hoshi is waving now, feeling a little bad for his quick temper, it's only his daughter's face looks so angry and the rain has gotten his face all wet and here she is taking his arm and looking into his bag and she's pulling it away from him, and he's fighting her, he won't let it go, not today, not with this storm, not when he'll need it to block out the noise.

霧島

They do not find Alec in Komachi, not in a river, not at the bottom of a gorge, not at home, and despite her certainty that he has not left her in this manner, Kanae goes along with the searching and the questions, she stays with the police officers and even though the weather is becoming very difficult, they are able to check the most likely places and still there is no sign of him, until suddenly, in the early evening, when she calls his cell phone, it seems that someone picks up.

"Alec? Is that you?" What rowdy crackle greets her question, or is that a breath? "Do you hear me?" She is speaking Japanese and English, trying all of their words, nothing seems to break through the static until the phone goes dead and the cheerful voice of a recorded message informs her that the phone has lost service, that they are very sorry for the inconvenience.

That evening the local news carries the story of the missing English teacher and Kanae watches the brief broadcast with her three children beside her at their home, each child touching her in some way, whether a foot or a hand or a shoulder, and then, when the broadcast is finished and the television personalities have returned to discussing the weather, Megumi, who cannot abide inactivity for too long, clicks off the television and stands up, announces that maybe he saw it.

"You mean if he were somewhere with a TV," says Naomi from her end of the sofa, and everyone's eyes turn to her, because all day she has been the most afraid of agreeing with Kanae's conviction that Alec is unharmed, instead she has avoided the discussion, left the room or turned away from the conversation, she has been crippled by sudden bouts of crying, and even mild-mannered Ken'ichi has grown angry with his sister, reminded her that she must be stronger than this.

Ken'ichi is the first to leave, ducking gently from the house with a word about wanting to get back to Etsuko and promising to return first thing in the morning, and then Megumi begins to gather her things, and Kanae follows Megumi right up to her car door, their faces sweating in the heat of the night, rain dropping on their heads, and they are staring at one another and Megumi says she heard the nurses speaking, she heard them whisper that Kanae hadn't been at the hospital until today, and she is asking her mother what did they mean.

She is such a wiry woman, Kanae is thinking, this girl-turned-mother, her body an arrow of movement and precision, and although her mouth is different now, a strict line across the small oval of her face, her eyes haven't yet gone hard, and in them she can see there is another Megumi layered beneath this older woman and if she could just pull one up from beneath the other, if she could just flip her daughter inside-out, they would all remember that young Megumi loved to laugh.

"Okāsan, why fight now? You never disagree about anything."

All that sky above her head, even with the thrashing trees and the moving clouds, she can see the moon, and her heart is beating too quickly with her sudden anger, this redness growing within. How can she explain when she cannot understand it herself. How she considers his life with her a promise, and that he is about to break it.

Her always-angry daughter is pulling her close now, like she were the child, and they stand together next to Megumi's car while the dark night swallows up the sound of Kanae's hard breathing, and Kanae waits as long as Megumi will let her, holding tight to the rigid grip of her daughter's thin arms, wanting Megumi's sharpness for her own now, knowing that she will need it, and there is a moment when she thinks she can hear Megumi crying, but the sound is so alien, so unbelievable, that she knows it must be a tree limb leaning into another or a bird swooping under the cover of a bush, and then they are straightening up, leaning away from each other, separate now, and Megumi's tiny face is solemn. Resigned.

Back inside and it is nearly midnight, but Kanae will not be sleeping this evening, not in her bed, not with the smell of Alec all around her, instead she is pacing the house, checking on Naomi who has taken something to help her sleep, checking the windows and listening to the creaking of the wood in the wind, and trying to see out into the darkness but the clouds have come down too low, there is no moon, there is only the black night and the drip of water racing down the glass.

When the house telephone rings she picks it up, fully angry again, knowing that it must be a policeman or the hospital, knowing that what they will tell her cannot possibly be true and how dare they disturb her so late in the evening, but it is only a quiet voice she hardly recognizes, it is only Fumikaze.

"I saw the news. About your husband."

She is holding a hand up, ready to block his approach.

"Did they . . . I mean, have you . . . do they know where he is?"

Kanae is opening her mouth, hoping that the action alone will get her voice to work, but it doesn't right away, and she stands there, mouth frozen, throat dry, until the silence grows too long and he is the one to speak again, he is telling her that he'll help, if he can, but she cannot allow this, and so she finds a single sentence to give him the apology he deserves.

"I wish I had never seen you again." Such a hard sentence for our Fumikaze to say, and even with these words, Kanae can tell he isn't really angry.

Her shame grows, she remembers from their childhood his willingness to surrender, if another child teased him, she was first to pinch an arm or push a body, she was his defender, and he was her quiet, shy friend.

"They should not have burdened you with his diagnosis. That must have been quite a shock."
"No, no one told me."
"You didn't know?"
"I knew when my husband knew."

My husband, she repeats, she says this word a few times, how strange that it should feel so alien on her tongue, 主人, *shujin*. The master of the house, and how funny that all she would have to do is lengthen the vowel, *shūjin*, *shūjin*, and the word becomes something else entirely, *prisoner* or *public*. 主人　囚人　衆人. How quickly something intimate and secret becomes its opposite.

"What I did was unforgivable—"

But he cuts her off and tells her that he hopes she will find her husband soon, that he is sorry for her trouble, and she can only cover the mouthpiece of the phone and refuse him the sob that rises in her throat, and they are hanging up like strangers.

This morning the day and the night are still fighting, the lines have been blurred by the rain and the clouds, and it looks like the light will be half-dying all day until this storm pushes its way to us and passes on, and for some time yet it will feel like night will go on forever, it will feel like the sun is never coming back to us, it will feel like our little island has been abandoned, thrown to the side of the ocean like an unwanted thing, a sacrifice to chaos and weather; this is when we must finish our preparations and so I am getting out the rolls of masking tape and climbing up on a step ladder to crisscross the windows all over the house, I am filling pots and pans and jars and thermoses with water, I am pulling the old camping toilet up from the basement and filling its reservoir for the day or so that the plumbing may be disturbed from an overflow of water to the sewers, and I am nailing blankets to the windows at the top of the house because these windows almost always break if the typhoon is big enough, and they have said it will be plenty big. And when all of this is done, I move to the kitchen to make *onigiri* from my leftover rice—I don't need much, I am just an old woman.

But the animals will need more from me and the shed must be made safer, it is a rickety structure and last year one of the walls shifted, so on with my coat and my gloves and I am out in the wind now and looking at this slapdash structure, at the angle of the wall against the tinny roof, and I am pacing around it and checking for loose boards and pushing against it with my hands, as if my hands would have the strength of the storm, and I must laugh at myself just a little, I am getting carried away, and then I remember there are some thin old ropes in Grandfather's cupboard and I can braid them and throw them over the shed roof and use them to anchor the sides of the building, like making this shed into a boat, an ark for these animals, and it only takes me an hour but when it is done I am pleased with my work, and if my grandfather were here he would give me that smile and that nod and I would know that he approved.

Now I must rest, just a little, and the wind is only becoming interesting, only yet a slight force, a nuisance, not yet dangerous, and so I sit in the garden for a moment, just outside my shed on an old stump, and the trees are turning a darker green and I ignore the whispers and echoes of this street and of Komachi, and I hear only the sounds of the evening and the hum of the insects as they are startled from their daytime hiding places, and now that smell of rain has deepened and already the wind is pulling gently at the house, pushing at any loose wooden shingles and reminding me about the badger, who should really stay with me for another day or two, but she will not manage the storm in her cage, she must be underground or she will turn on herself, biting and hurting, and all of my work would be for nothing; so the storm has decided for me, it is time to give her up to her life.

The shed erupts with nervous scrambling when I enter through the doorway; the hares excited and hopping around, rubbing up against the sides of their cages, and the hawk is sliding along his perch, trying to unfurl his wings and closing them tight against his bandage, and the lizard is moving carefully over his rocks and even the butterflies—yes, they can be healed—are flitting about, because with the open door comes the scent of the forest again and they have not forgotten it is their home.

I am stopping now before the badger's cage and she is watching me and I am watching her, and this is the first time she has been quiet enough to see me and when the understanding passes between us, she lies down on her belly and holds her head at attention and waits for me to unlock the cage door, and when it is open and I have stepped aside, she rises to her feet and stares at me once more.

"Go," I tell her. "Go on into the forest."

She is past me in a flash, slipping out the open door and off into the field, racing with her nearly healed legs and her head up to sniff the many scents of the open air and the forest and the running water just a few more bounds away, and her freedom is an exquisite thing to encounter, a healing done properly, even if that limp will endanger her for the rest of her days, she will be slower than necessary and she may not make it across a road as quickly as she will need to, because we humans are sloppy in our driving, careless with our speeds and the power and weight of our machines, and I am moving further into the field now, following her, hoping for a last glimpse of her stripe as it slips into the grass, hoping she might stop where the forest begins and let me admire her one last time, but I'm scanning the tree trunks and she is already gone, already following the scent of the wild persimmons, already thinking of a den, and I can only close my eyes and let her go, I can only wish her well for as many seasons as she has left in these woods.

霧島

What Kanae doesn't know is that Fumikaze was standing outside the love hotel and searching for his car when two prostitutes were coming out, ready to go home, and what tired women they were, all that heavy make-up washed away, faces too plain for their latex skirts and high-heeled boots, but they offered him a ride to find his car and he accepted, sitting stiffly in the back seat, eyes on the road and making small talk about the rain and the wind and the women were yawning and he was thinking they had frightened each other, he and Kanae, he was thinking they had done something very rash and of course she had run away, who could blame her, it isn't every day you reconnect with someone and find such passion.

So very quickly he was back inside his car, and instead of driving north along the coast, instead of finding a sensible hotel to weather out the storm, he has driven into the mountains, toward Komachi, and rented himself a room, not at one of the great, gleaming *onsen* hotels for whom he works, but at a worn down *ryokan* on the back-side of one of our more modest mountain peaks, and because there were only two inns still open because of the impending storm, he chose the older, the less distinguished of the two. Our gentle Fumikaze told himself he wanted to look at property in Komachi, told himself it might be cheaper than Miyazaki, told himself he might like retiring in the place where he grew up, a kind of full-circle movement, and he told himself it had nothing to do with her.

And then, from his room at the inn, he saw the news report about the missing English teacher, and of course Kanae was in the photo they flashed across the screen, such a handsome couple, and he learned more in that short news broadcast than he had at their two dinners and one night together, such a successful family—an academic son, an artistic daughter, another daughter in business, and there it was, the words plain as he could read, The Language Lab, one of Komachi's most community-oriented companies, even if the police were sounding pessimistic, and he cannot stop the thought that maybe Kanae did not lie to him exactly, maybe she was already a widow but didn't really know it.

It is morning now and Fumikaze is sitting over a late breakfast he has asked to be able to eat in the garden of the *ryokan* because it is one of the best he has ever seen, and there is just enough shelter from the rain under one long slanting eave that juts out from the side of the house, and so he is raising his chopsticks again and again, resting his eyes on the perfectly smooth paving stones and the small pond frothy with rain and the darting movements of several fat koi.

Across the garden the old owner has got her hands busy with twine and burlap sacks, tying up the plants and fastening the garden chairs, he nods to her and she raises a small curved hand in return, but what really struck him about the newscast was how quick it all was, how only the slimmest details of these lives were given, everyone a name and a profession, but what did all that have to do with losing a husband, losing a father, it was all so neat and prompt and clean, and then the newscaster was back at the typhoon and computer mock-ups of swirling clouds and bright colors and there it was at the edge of the screen, the line of Kyūshū and the water rising over the sea wall along the Pacific coast.

He sips his bowl of tea, he can still feel the tightness in his abdominal muscles and biceps from two nights before, and he knows it was hard on him, this lovemaking at his age, he should take care to get more exercise, and he is thinking that she enjoyed it, he believes she was not simply out of her mind with grief, because she was with him, she was in that room with him, she touched him, too.

Idiot, he is saying, placing his tea bowl back on the tray with a forceful click, no, he is thinking, no, he cannot understand, would a wife who loved her husband do such a horrible thing, he wants to be sure, he wants to make a firm judgment and file these thoughts away, but there is so much uncertainty, it is said that love will make you crazy, make you imbalanced, he has never wanted this, he has only ever wanted to feel safe, to spread his safeness across another pair of shoulders.

The wind has shifted and the rain is now splashing his slippered feet, adding its wetness to his empty tea cup, and across the garden the owner stops and lifts her head, looks at the sky. It's now, isn't it? The storm is here, she says, and then she is yelling out for the kitchen boy to remove Fumikaze's tray, and the wind is scooping through the garden now, pushing at the flaps of his *yukata* robe and sending his napkin into the pond and a bright white koi is already dragging it down beneath the water and he stands there, getting wet, thinking of Kanae again, wondering where she is and if she's out now again with the police, looking for her husband, and everyone must be getting so worried, maybe they have found his body, but he reminds himself it is none of his business, he must leave Komachi as soon as the storm blows over, and he hopes it will all go quickly.

The doorbell is ringing suddenly, and the owner looks up from her busy work, cocking her head as if she isn't sure what the sound is, but she stands then, brushing her hands down her apron and bowing to Fumikaze once more, leaving the tree she's been wrapping so carefully, and so he walks over and leans down to finish it for her, getting all wet now, but wraps the twine around and around, pulling it tight, and when he's finished, he closes his eyes, her skin was not as soft as he thought it would be, not as he had imagined it—he hadn't imagined it often, but enough, a few times over the years he had thought of her, pictured her face, dreamed of a chance meeting, but this is what old bachelors do, they make things up, then they make the best of things.

霧島

When Kanae wakes in the morning, she goes out into the garden directly, still in her nightgown, and the rain is coming down hard and fast—typhoon rain is thick and unforgiving, like the ocean has been sucked up into the wind and hurled back in strings of hard silver beads toward the earth; Kanae just stands and lets these thick ropes of water lash at her, and when she's cold enough, when her skin is turning red, then blue, and she is shivering and her heart is racing because of the force of the storm, she stumbles back inside.

There is a note for her in the kitchen, written in Megumi's hand, the ink is always very dark because she presses so firmly with the nib of the pen, and she wonders how Megumi got back here so quickly this morning, and then she wonders again about Jun and why Megumi hasn't brought him—but the note doesn't tell her about her grandson, the note only reads: *Naomi and I went to the store. Be back soon.*

Her daughters have teamed up to take care of her and the idea makes her cringe a little, because they have decided that she needs their help, and while there is love in this gesture, there is also pity and there is the fact that no one will experience Alec's loss the way Kanae will, and already her children have understood this, and so she crumples the note. Also, in Megumi's toughly-scribbled lines there is an uncomfortable reversal, for the first time in her life Kanae isn't the first to worry whether the family will have candles if the electricity goes out, if there is enough food prepared and stored, if the hot water tank is full, she isn't the first to think and plan for all these sundry details of an impending typhoon, because her daughters have taken over so completely, there is no room left for her.

She slides to the floor of the *genkan*, kneeling beside the neat stacks of shoes and slippers, near the welcome Buddha on his little podium with his beatific smile and protruding belly, and quickly, with just a little snatch of her arm out and back, she takes a pair of Alec's shoes from his side of the shelf and stuffs them inside her nightgown, against her skin, pressing the leather and the stiff shoelaces, and little clods of dirt from the soles scratch her skin but she cradles this pair of shoes as her sorrow takes over.

Let us give her this moment, let us turn away, because the relief in letting herself cry will be ugly for us to look it, we can step outside the door so as not to hear her whimpering, we can stand here a moment feeling the force of the wind and the sound of the crashing up in the forest, and when she's ready, it won't be long, Kanae has always been the stronger one, we can step back inside and see that she has already gotten herself up off the floor, she has dropped Alec's shoes to the floor and she is dashing through the house to her bedroom.

She will need to be dressed appropriately, she is thinking, safely is what she means, and I am happy now, this is the Kanae I have always known, now watch her leave her wet nightgown in the bathtub, watch her strip off her sodden underwear and camisole and now she is racing back to the closet, a whir of flesh and determination, and she is pulling on clean, dry underwear, a sturdy bra, an undershirt, she is taking one of Alec's old shirts, a flannel he used to wear to work in the garden, and it's incredibly soft, and she puts it over a cotton sweater and pulls on a pair of her jeans—up on a shelf with the winter clothing, she finds a hat and a scarf and then back to the *genkan* for her raincoat, and then she is pushing candles and plastic bags and a flashlight into her pockets, and before she leaves she fills a small backpack with a change of clothes for Alec, just in case.

She is standing a moment, hesitating, but then she decides, watch her now as she rolls her bicycle out of the garage, leaving her car in the driveway so that her children will first believe she is just lying down somewhere in the house, they will not go looking for her right away, and now she is tying the strings of her raincoat hood firmly around her neck and heading out into the relentless wall of rain. The wind is strong and she must push against it, and at the edge of the neighborhood, she passes her daughters driving back home but they don't recognize her, they don't even look twice at her small hunkered shape behind the handlebars, and she gets a brief glimpse of their tense faces through the windshield, Megumi is driving, squinting against the rain, and Naomi is holding a small hand to her mouth, eyes wide.

This is the moment when Kanae begins speaking to Alec again, the moment she forgives him for leaving her, the moment she accepts that she has wasted some of the short time they will have together, and in her careful progress down the road, she begins a dialogue with him in whispers; in the familiar hushed tone of their intimate conversations, (isn't this how they spoke when the children were sleeping, or when in public and something private must be said), she explains what she is doing, she gives him a litany of her smallest actions—how she must push on the pedals, hold the handlebar with a firm grip, change gears for a slight rise—she speaks to him as though he were right beside her on his own bike, she speaks to him as though giving him these details of her movements is what will get them through the storm.

霧島

Alec is thanking the old woman but she continues to hover at the door, she is still astounded by his Japanese, giving him compliment after compliment, and she does not remember him, surely she would not still be staring at him if she knew who he was, knew that he has lived his entire life here in these mountains, and so he wants to snap at her, he wants to show her his passport, tell her that he's practically as Japanese as she is, that this is his home and he is tired of being told in gestures and glances that it isn't, he wants to tell her to get herself out of this small place, to see the world, to know that travel isn't so difficult anymore and there is nothing so special about him, but instead he says:

"I don't want to be any trouble."
"Oh, you're no trouble. It's just with the storm . . . the wiring in this old house is terrible. We may not have any hot water this evening. Our food may not be up to standards."

And she is bustling from the night table to the window, back to the dresser to wipe at an invisible speck of dirt and then over to the closet, and the whole time the lights are flickering a bit, the lamps are humming over their heads. She smoothes the sleeves of his jacket on its hanger, slides the door closed and then she is finally bowing to him and shuffling away out the door, her back hunched, her head tipped to the side as if her ears were leading her down to the first floor and the other guests, to her small staff and into the kitchen.

The rain is still beating against the roof of the *ryokan* but it seems to be softening a little, and Alec listens to the steady thrumming, noting everything about the spare room about him, the neat rectangles of *tatami* and the shadows thrown by the flowers and this tall thin vase in the alcove, the way the bottom of the hanging scroll taps lightly against the wall as the house sways just a bit in the wind. The furniture is simple and sturdy but everything has faded and one of the pillow cases of the cushions is much too bright, altogether in the wrong taste, much too modern for this run-down inn, and he takes it up and crushes it between his hands while he paces the room, looking for somewhere to hide it, to get it out of his sight, what a horrible object, he won't be forced to look at it, no, how tacky, how cheap, and he jumps toward the closet, stuffing it toward the back beneath the extra futon and when it is good and hidden, when he is no longer touching the stiff fabric, he can sit down and breathe a little easier.

Alec cannot remember if this was their room, it could have been, this could have been the small space they shared for three days, the length of honeymoon they could afford at the time, going only so far as this steep hill outside Komachi and this traditional *ryokan*, now fallen out of style compared to the bigger *onsen* hotels that draw tourists to our mountains each year. They did not put a foot outside the inn, took all their meals in their room, crept down into the guest house's cavernous bathing room in the early hours of dawn before any of the other guests were awake and only once went out onto the balcony to watch a meteor shower, and so Alec should be able to remember whether this was their room, he should remember its corners and shadows, should remember what it looked like with the futon spread out across the floor and the window half-cracked open, and the color of his new wife's skin lit with sun through the glass, and the taste of her and the slide of their bodies and the shape of their happiness, yes, he should be able to feel the hard permanent edges of their happiness as it grew between them in this small space.

"I am still strong," he is saying, testing the sound of his voice now in the dusty air, how it rumbles below the rattling sound of the window and the knock of a branch at the side of the wall, and then the sound of a crash reaches him from outside, and he is on his feet, only wincing a little at the pain that ignites in the trunk of his body at this swift movement, he is pushing back the drapes and sliding open the window, and down in the courtyard the old woman is hovering over a young man in a cooking apron who is trying to right a trash can that has fallen over. The old woman's kimono is soaking wet, sticking to the back of her legs and keeping her from walking properly, and she is shouting to the young man to tie the cans with rope to a tree in the center of the garden, and the rain is dripping off her face and her eyes are fluttering against the water and the wind.

And Alec is shouting in English now, shouting down to these two figures below him, his arm stretched out into the rain, his face fixed in a grimace, and he is telling them that he's still strong, that he's stronger than they think, and they are staring back up at him, faces frozen, mouths gaping, arms and hands thrown up to block the rain—and for just a second too long all three of these people stay perfectly still and they could be statues, or carved puppets, petrified, silent, unmoving.

Organized Convection

Kanae holds her legs still, letting the bicycle carry her forward with its momentum, it isn't so hard really, pushing herself through the wind, the storm feels like it is slowing, maybe it is beginning to run through its course, and so she pedals again, and her legs strain less, and the flats of her thighs and her wrists are soaked with water where her raincoat offers no protection, and the air against her face is still cold, but she's warm, her damp underclothes are pressed against her and are humid from her exertions.

Our Komachi is not so big and there are not many opportunities for doing what the hospital and the authorities suspect that Alec has done—a train, the bridge, the river—and so she has ridden out toward the big bridge that connects old-town Komachi with its modern neighborhoods on the other side of the swift Komachi River.

"He wouldn't," she is saying, as we're all saying. "He wouldn't."

Still, she peddles on, and she doesn't check the train station because the inter-village trains are not running today anyway, not until the storm passes, and if there had been an accident this morning, she would already know, the whole town would know by the flashing light above the train relay cables. In all the years she has lived in Komachi there have been four suicides by train, and each time there is a piercing wail and a flashing light at each track interchange, a modern incantation for the departed soul, for the few hours until the tracks are cleared and it is safe for the trains to run again.

She bumps along the bike path on the left bank of the river, watching carefully for areas where the river may be overflowing and twisting her handlebars to negotiate the gusts of wind, several times she is blown sideways and must stop her fall with a foot dropped to the ground, and there are places her bicycle crosses through a few inches of water as the level of the river continues to rise, and so she keeps her eyes on the rough concrete, checking for debris that could knock her off her bike, checking the choppy surface of the water until she is stopped in surprise by the fat silver bodies of fish suddenly jumping up and into the air, the flash and arc of their bodies rising sharply and then twisting and plunging back into the muddy tangle of swollen river.

"Alec is not here," she says, speaking aloud because it calms her, because the sound of her voice reminds her that she is here, right now, she is on this bike, despite her cold slippery hands, despite the risk of falling, despite the risk of something falling on her, and she is no longer running away from Alec, but toward him. "Alec would not do this to me."

There in the river is a piece of red plastic, maybe a rain coat, but it doesn't matter because it isn't Alec's, it is the wrong color, and once she sees this first item, she notices a wash of other personal items, pitching and rolling through the churning water: a baseball cap, an umbrella, a cardboard box, what looks like a book—she watches the water rising even further, these items coming toward her, the water coming up to touch her pedals and she knows she will have to get away from the river now, and Kanae bows her head, says a prayer for the first time in years, an honest prayer, focused and careful, her physical body turning inward, turning away from the storm, and for a few seconds she is calm.

But the feeling is instinctively addictive and she gets her bicycle moving forward and away from the river path, out toward the wide street, now with renewed hope, because isn't this what generations of Komachi citizens have done in their own private moments of terror? And why should she be any different? Why shouldn't she call on these gods?

"I am no longer like them," she once said, in the early years of her marriage. "I have moved off-center, I am somewhere in between. I can't be exactly like you, Alec, but I have stopped being like everyone else."

"We're in our own crazy boat, aren't we? Rowing alongside them but in a parallel river."

Once they even considered leaving Japan, moving to England or America because they wondered if their children deserved this kind of opportunity, wondered how it would change them, and now Kanae cannot remember which of them, was it her, was it Alec, eventually kept the plan from going forward, but she does know one thing, she knows they are being punished for the way they secretly enjoyed feeling a little different from everyone else.

"That isn't true," Alec would surely say. "I cannot believe that people would be punished for their happiness, what a hideous god that would be."

Years ago, a month ago, a week ago, she would have agreed with him, and they would have discussed this guilt and these religions and why the two were such eager partners, and they would have compared notes on the way they were each raised, descriptions of family traditions and conversations with parents and friends, and they might have even discussed their own children and whether that legacy of thinking might have been passed along, they would have asked each other, as they often have, how their mixed culture household had influenced Megumi, Naomi, and Ken'ichi, and how now, as adults, these three were different from their peers.

Kanae is heading toward the other bridge now on the east side of town and is cutting through Komachi's entertainment district, a gray and shadowy place of unlit neon signs and narrow streets, windows boarded up to wait out the storm, and this is when she hears the crash, and at first she thinks she is imagining it, that she has created this noise in her mind from a cache of worry that is suddenly too big to carry within, that she has somehow tossed it from herself, thrown it down onto the street and can now watch her anger and fear explode. But then she sees the tipped signboard hanging from the side of a karaoke bar and she sees the traffic light smashed on the ground, and there are still sparks shooting up into the air, splutters of light and energy, and all she can do is jerk her handlebars to the left and turn down into an alley where the wind is blocked, where only papers are blowing; when she reaches the other side of this alley, she stops—the town is silent, no one is out on the streets, there are wet papers, flyers, and other debris, being flicked from lamppost to tree trunk to mailbox, the electrical lines are swaying in the sky above Kanae's head, and she watches them, watches the big box of another traffic light sway forward and backward and she steadies herself on the alley wall, legs burning from the exercise, and she knows that in a very short amount of time all of her conversations with Alec will be just like the one she's just finished—one-sided and pretend. Without answers.

A flick of an ear, a careful twist of the head, Komachi is alive tonight with stories and voices, and so we move in closer again to the Chester household, this time to Megumi who is watching her sister seated on the couch, watching Naomi's half-frozen face, stricken with fear since their visit to the hospital the day before, and Megumi can hardly stand to stay in the same room with her.

"Nao-chan, I'm going to see if I can get Mrs. Kenta, I want to see if she's taken Jun over to her parents' house."

Naomi looks up, her eyes wide. "I hope they're not out on the road right now."

"The storm is stronger here, it might not even be raining hard yet in Kumamoto."

But no one is answering at Mrs. Kenta's apartment, and Megumi cannot get the woman's cell phone to connect, and here it comes, the sharp glitter shard of irritation, Megumi's special form of panic—she should have brought Jun with her, what was she thinking leaving him so far away from her during a typhoon?

"No answer?" Naomi has followed Megumi into the kitchen, is already rubbing the knuckles of one hand with the other, kneading and stretching the skin.

"I'll go check the shutters are all latched upstairs. Go lie down, everything is going to be fine."

Megumi can feel her sister's eyes on her back as she hurries from the room, and it makes her even more angry, because Naomi's constant worrying is exhausting, what good does it do to give all your concerns the same quantity of anxiety? Naomi has never learned how to parcel out her fear, how to distribute her apprehension into a variety of shapes and sizes and allocate them appropriately, but Megumi knows how to do this and by the time she reaches the top of the stairs she is feeling nearly smug, proud of how well she can apportion her emotions and how she knows to save her energy for important fears.

She is looking around now, surprised to see how little this house has changed since the years she lived here with the rest of the family, her parents have not rearranged, have not made Ken'ichi's larger room into a study, or made Megumi's small room into a guest bedroom. As they were when she was a child, the bedrooms are all clustered at one end of the long hallway, a study and a family room at the other—it is a big house by Japanese standards, it is nearly luxurious and definitely sturdily built, because the sounds of the typhoon are so quiet here in this interior hallway, and she is looking at the solid wood beneath her feet and remembering how much she loved to run the length of these floors, sliding in her socks into the study to catch her father napping on the sofa or her mother reading a book, and Naomi or Ken were always at her heels, too timid to run and slide but anxious to follow her in search of their parents.

Megumi stops now, hovering at the edge of the large family room, she will always associate this house with both of her parents, the space is such a mixture of their two personalities, a blend of east and west even if the décor is mostly Japanese and it strikes her as strange how traditionally styled her parents have kept the house, to an outside eye this house is so stereotypically Japanese and yet their family has always been a blend, not quite Japanese, not quite Western, and she runs her fingertips along the edge of a painting, it is one of her own, one she no longer cares for, it looks childish to her, the feeling so boldly stated, and she closes her eyes because she cannot yet imagine her mother living here alone, no, it will be too big for her by herself, she will give it up quickly, she will not want to share the space with all of her memories. And then Megumi is angry again, swiftly, satisfyingly so, because she should not be able to imagine this future so quickly, she should not be able to see her father vanishing so easily and yet he has already started to thin and disappear.

The beep of her cell phone startles her forward out of the hall-way and into the family room, her knees down onto the humid

116

tatami—it is Mrs. Kenta and Megumi breathes deeply with relief, savoring the earthy smell of the woven floor, "We are at my parents' house," Mrs. Kenta is saying. "It is safer here, there is no flooding expected." And Megumi is agreeing, her anger set aside, for now, and asking to speak to her son.

"Are you playing with Grandpa Kenta?"
Jun is laughing, "We're killing the invaders, the aliens haven't got a chance!"

Megumi reminds him to be polite and mind Mrs. Kenta and her parents, and she tells him she'll be back to pick him up tomorrow but he doesn't seem the least bit concerned that he won't see her this evening.

"Can I have ice cream?"
"If Mrs. Kenta offers."
"We had some at lunch, I just wanted to be sure."
"You're a rascal, be good. And, Jun, you're my best boy."
"Always!"

They hang up then and Megumi holds tight to her cell phone for a few extra seconds, hearing the echo of his little boy voice, already so confident, and she is aware that she is known for being assertive herself, for speaking her mind, even if it isn't very feminine of her, not that she cares. But Jun's assertiveness is different, a variety of self-assuredness he hasn't gotten from her, and although she would never tell this to anyone, she is certain it comes from Jun's father because everyone knows that Americans have confidence and optimism in their blood.

Mrs. Kenta asked her once, as have so many others, and as politely as possible, whether Jun ever saw his father, and when Megumi replied that the two had never met, Mrs. Kenta was either too embarrassed or too discreet to inquire any further, not that it would have done her any good, Megumi has never told anyone how she became pregnant with Jun, especially not her parents nor her siblings, all of whom begged for the truth when she announced she would be having a child, alone, on her own.

She has imagined telling them many times, a casual announcement over dinner, an easy phrase tossed into a conversation and which would throw them all into a stunned silence: These American sperm clinics are really great, and Hawaii isn't so far, really... and it was really easy.

Oh, Megumi, what a lie this would be, nothing about having Jun was easy for you, you were terrified, you worried you would lose the baby, you worried you would hate the baby, and you went through labor for thirty-two hours, completely on your own at the hospital in Kumamoto because you refused to call your parents when you'd started to feel the labor pains and all because you believed you knew what it would be like, you knew they would be happy for you, but you were too afraid to see their own happiness, too afraid to see your parents, their couplehood, strengthened by the birth of their first grandchild, and it was what you were fighting against, isn't it? You wanted to create something you could love as much as your parents have always loved each other, you'd promised yourself this, years ago when you were still a very young woman, you'd promised that if you ever had any children you would love them more than anyone else, that any child deserved this, and that you would put your child first.

霧島

From inside the house, the sounds of a typhoon are always loud—the wind clawing at the trees, clawing at the shutters and the roof tiles, whistling between the cars and the houses, hurtling bits of debris against the walls and windows, and I know it will be quieter outside, even now when the storm wall is approaching us fast, running up the sides of our mountains and settling in over our small town, and because of all this noise, I can no longer hear anything and I must brave the winds to check the forest with my eyes, to make sure the animals have all tucked themselves away, to make sure I am not needed. And so off I go beneath layers of cloth and plastic, meant to keep me dry but also to protect me from the sticks and bits of other people's lives that will go flying through the air, and the worst part is the trek across the open field of my garden because I am such a small woman and the wind threatens to knock me over, but once I reach the stand of *sugi* and once I am on the trail, it is easier because these tree trunks are thick and the water is not running over the ground, not softening the earth around the tree trunks, and so maybe we will flood a little, later perhaps, but the ground will not give way. We are protected.

We learn in school that typhoons love Japan, that ten or more a year approach our islands, and that most of these storms make landfall in the south, poor Okinawa, but here on Kyūshū we also have more than our share, we are often bombarded with these winds and this rain, and while we worry over these storms, while we fret and prepare and discuss what will happen and what has happened in the past, and while we complain to our politicians about the measures being taken and the measures being ignored, we also secretly love these typhoons, just a little, we love them because they test our spirit and our strength, and each and every time we make it through—we have been knocked down a little, yes, we have suffered, we have been inconvenienced, but against these storms, we have always won.

I am slow to climb the trail and I even slip once or twice, but I make it and I am proud of my wiry arms and sturdy thin legs, I am checking around my patch of forest, testing the trees and listening for the animals and watching the way the water is running down the little stream—it is swollen, yes, but it is still only a stream—and

119

everything is as it should be, the tree limbs are wild and the wind is reminding me of my own smallness and the animals are silent and hidden. So I sit for a moment to catch my breath in the hollow at the base of the biggest oak tree, and I wish I could stay here, huddled and warm and dry and certain that this weather would pass over me eventually, but I must return to my home and experience this storm like everyone else, it is a choice I must honor.

So back on the path and gripping the muddy rocks and tree roots where I can, because going down is always harder than climbing up, with my feet slick on the mud and the rain pushing me from behind, and then there is a crack up above, a sound like thunder, the reluctant splitting of wood from wood, and then another crack, and the trees are crying out at their lost limbs and twisting in anger against the wind, and I must get out of the way until they have calmed, and so I am scurrying just a little further down the trail, and ducking into the old shrine, it is nothing more than a rock ledge with an overhang, but the debris won't reach me here, not if I scoot myself back against the rock and I wait and it's terrible, this cracking and tearing above me and so I turn away from the violence, I turn toward the moss-covered statues at my feet, a little row of them, not any higher than my knee, but what is left of their round faces is so solemn and so peaceful and I stare back at them until my own worries are settled.

Not many people in Komachi remember this old shrine—there are no stone steps leading up to its entrance, no building for monks to visit and where people may come to pray, there is nothing but this ledge, this row of statues and a wooden box set into the ledge of the rock, with doors that were once painted red, and a drawer in which to leave offerings, but those of us who grew up in this neighborhood, who love or loved to walk in these woods, have often stopped by to pause in the quiet of its shelter, to wonder at these unnamed and soon-to-be faceless statues, and there are even a few people who believe they are the only ones to know about this place, and they have left parts of themselves, secret wishes and vows, made from folded slips of paper and pieces of money in the offering box. One such couple was so beautiful in their solitude, so honest in their communion, so free from the prying eyes that usually marked their public appearance, and this is years ago now, that it would not have been right for an old woman to break that silence and announce her presence, it was better to leave them alone and let them keep the memory of this little shrine to themselves.

I run my fingers along the heads of the statues and wonder again who carved them and what people or monks were their model and then I am off back onto the path because the wind has quieted a little, has left the trees to their armless grieving and I can move a little faster and soon the path is leveling out and reaching the road, and I am crossing the road and slipping into my back garden—I am soaked through, how did I not notice it? I must hurry now and change my clothes, get inside my house and warm up, because I am still an old woman and it would not do to let this storm get the better of me.

霧島

The *ryokan* will break in this storm, thinks Alec, because already the power has gone out, already a window has broken somewhere, he could hear the old woman and her lonely housekeeper discussing how to patch it up, and he almost stood up and went to them, wanting to offer his help—because have they even prepared?—but when he tried to stand up from the cushions on the floor, he had to sit back down again, panting, moving a hand to the small of his back, pressing against the heat and the throb and the pain of this everywhere that is no longer medicated.

"Seventeen children," he told her once, from maybe this very room. "I was hoping you'd want sixty, I'll be pregnant every year of my life."

He remembers reaching for the smooth skin of her belly, the taut line of flesh between each hip bone. "No, no, let's forget that. No children. I won't change an inch of you."

"I'll grow fat anyway. You've been warned, you've met my mother."

He bit her upper arm, licked the tip of her elbow. "Then I'll eat you for breakfast and lunch and dinner. Every day."

But that was then and this is now, and this room is dark and the wind is rushing at the side of the building and there is a crash in the courtyard and then the hurried scurry of feet along the hallway.

"Is everything okay in here?" This from the old woman, she has entered his room without knocking. "Your lights are off as well? Come downstairs then, we've got a lantern in the dining room, it is the most protected room, and we're going to serve some lunch."

Alec follows her out the door, sliding along the wooden floor in his socks, he has forgotten his slippers and Kanae would tell him he is behaving like a dotty old man, she would tell him to find something else to do, to read a book, write a card, pot a plant, and she would be somewhere keeping her hands busy, setting an example, but Alec is walking down the stairs now, listening to the rain on the roof and staring at the papery skin of the old woman's neck, and he is wondering if they've got it all wrong, because this time he is pretty sure that a busy pair of hands will not solve their problem.

Downstairs in the dining room is a man about his age, and they bow to one another, and the man stares at Alec just a beat too long, as Japanese people sometimes do, but Alec doesn't mind, he is already turning away, yes, turning away from our Fumikaze, already looking for a magazine, something to keep his attention until they bring in the lunch, so that he won't just stand there holding his abdomen and tiptoeing around and looking up at the roof. The structure of the *ryokan* is creaking and groaning, the trees are swaying over the skylight, and Alec chooses a low table and thanks the old woman for her pot of tea, and Fumikaze has stopped staring and has followed the old woman back into the hallway, from which Alec can still hear their conversation and he cannot help it, he has nothing better to do, he is listening.

There is some question of Fumikaze returning to town.
"Certainly not right now, sir, it's much too dangerous."
"It's rather important, so—"
"It can't last much longer, you really should wait—"

The man's voice lowers, and Alec is flicking through the pages of a catalog, reading about the amenities of various *onsen* hotels in the region, and he hears the old woman's short gasp of surprise, the mention of the word "teacher" and now the other man has said "hospital" and so, without waiting even a second he is dropping the catalog and pushing himself to his knees, never mind the round press of pain, the crimp at his side, he shouts to them in the hallway.

"I can hear you!"

What a silence then—even the storm seems to have been startled, and then he is standing, nevermind the tremble in his legs, nevermind the flush of fever that is rising in his cheeks, and he is walking to these people in the hallway, and how silly he must look, he thinks, towering over this gentle man and this gentle old woman with his oversized limbs and pale hair, but he hadn't expected the news of his situation to travel so quickly.

"There is some question about my health? Is that a problem?"
The old woman has bowed her head. How demure. How resigned.
But our Fumikaze is frowning now, embarrassed, hesitant to begin a conflict, to do anything but nod his head and tuck his disappointment and scurry away, but he stops himself. This is too important, this is worth fighting through. "I was sorry to hear of your illness, Mr. Chester."

Alec blinks. This man has spoken to him in English.

"Excuse my . . . um, please forgive my direct speech. I understand there is little time."

Now there is a question of hallucination, and Alec is pinching his arm a little and looking from the man to the window, back to the man, and shaking his head, looking in on his rational brain. Such perfect English . . . and Shingo did not mention the possibility of hallucination.

"Do I know you?"

But Fumikaze has moved away, is seated now in a chair by the entrance and is clasping both hands around one raised knee, he is not looking at Alec, but up at the ceiling, he has closed his eyes and all around them the storm is beating on, beating against the building, pushing at these structures, our feeble shelters and buildings, all of them in its way.

"You were not a student of mine. I would have remembered your excellent English."

A quick bow of his head, and then the man jumps a little in his seat as the front door rattles. "I have traveled a lot. English is a very practical language." And then he is looking at Alec, he is determined, he is not thinking of himself. "Sensei. You were on the news. They have put out a search party."

No, no, this is silly, and Alec is shaking his head, he is telling this man that they have better things to do, what with the storm and all, what with the rivers that will overflow and the possibility of landslides . . .

"There is no reason to be looking for me at a time like this."

But Fumikaze will not let him carry on, and he says, now in Japanese, now with the ease of a man returning to himself. "Sensei . . . your family . . . your family is looking for your body."

霧島

Today the hospital has become the beating heart of our little town, the injuries have begun to come in—small ones from broken glass and from slipping in the rain, and a large one when Mr. Kōno's back door blew in on him and knocked him into his kitchen table— and so there are extra nurses on duty tonight, and even though it was discussed and debated, they have asked young Nurse Noriko to come in and help, even if she might not be able to perform her job correctly, her mind is elsewhere you see, her spirit doesn't come to us without complications.

And here she is at the nursing station, they have asked her to maintain the floor, keep the paperwork sorted because this is always a problem on a busy day when more patients are coming in than going out, and so she is sorting the intake stickers and checking the files, she is making piles of folders in the box they use when they cannot file them right away in the large file room, and when the piles are neatly arranged, when the box is tucked under the desk, well, then she begins making visits to patient rooms and asking all the right questions, and none of the patients can even guess that she hasn't heard their answers, that she is scribbling the name of her boyfriend in all the empty boxes on her paperwork.

"Please take care of yourself," she says, bowing and smiling at the door as she backs out of each room, and then she turns on her heel and goes to the next.

And the patients are so pleased with her attentiveness, they feel so lucky to be in such good hands, especially today, when it is more than inconvenient to be sick, or worse, to have been injured by this terrible storm.

On her way from the women's corridor to the men's corridor, she must walk through the main lobby and she can see the emergency room entrance, the blinking lights have not stopped blinking today, and just now they are bringing in another person on a stretcher, one more hurt body to add to the tally from today, this time an older woman from one of the farms on the outskirts of town, who slipped in her garden while trying to cover her vegetable patch with a tarp, and the medics are sliding in all of the mud they've tracked in, and the nurses are calling for a janitor as the woman's arm slips off the stretcher, limp and dripping water, and there is a great commotion because this woman should only be a little shaken up, it was only a sliced finger, a bruised hip and maybe a strain, her life shouldn't be a question, but now we are asking it, and Nurse Noriko freezes as the alarm rings again, but this time it's the generator because the wall of the storm is upon us and the strength of the wind is much too much for our wires. The hospital goes black.

The children are crying and the mothers are shushing, an old man is laughing and ready to tell the story of the great typhoon of '21—the hospital lobby has rarely been this packed, this animated, and everyone is at the windows now, watching the black line of clouds through the rain, this is the storm's most furious moment and even the medics stop to pause, hardly a breathlong, because this woman needs chest compressions and they are wheeling her down a hallway, still slipping in the mud, especially in the dark, and the lights flicker, but only a flicker because the generator hasn't come on like it should, not right away, so people are shouting, a maintenance man running, and then—a crackle, a snap, there is light.

But Noriko has gone outside and she is standing in the overfull parking lot, in her pink uniform and that croissant-shaped hat, and there is water lashing against her legs and her hair has come free and the hat is now gone, let's watch it fly off into the wind, and the whole lobby is turned toward her, the news of her tragedy rippling quickly through the people.

"Yes, it's terrible."
"And he's so young, and she's nothing but a girl."
"Are they sure he won't wake up?"

And why isn't anyone going out to her?

The storm wall is coming, it's descending down from the sky, this noon sky without a sun, only these clouds and this wind, and Noriko is thinking of Masa, her boyfriend in his own hospital, with his own tubes and his injured brain, and the question is whether to let him go on, and they are waiting for her to decide if she will give him up, because she was supposed to have him for the rest of her life. But this isn't a fair question for a girl of her age, because the rest of her life is so long, and so she's passed it along to this storm, she is waiting for her answer, for the wind to push her over or take her away, for someone to make this decision in her stead, how on earth can they ask it of her—parents and family alike, they think she should be the one to decide to keep holding onto this young man whose brain has stopped working but whose body, a young man's body, is strong enough to go on.

And here it comes upon her, the full force of the wind, the first eyewall slamming down on her, on her little pink uniform, see it molded to her, see her tiny body, and she is blown against a first car, and there is a gasp in the lobby, and now other medics are running, picking up mud from the floor onto their once-clean shoes, and racing to catch her, because she's being slammed against another car, and the men are holding onto one another, and onto the wheel rims of the cars, cutting their hands on the metal, fingers straining on plastic, and they are crouched low to the ground to keep themselves safe. They reach her eventually, where she's wedged beneath the bumper of a third car, half on purpose because she is still young enough that something inside her does not want to die, and they gather her up just as the eyewall passes on, just as the wind drops completely, and she is so small really, and they will carry her back into the hospital, it's easy now, what with the stopping of the wind and the chain of bodies that has formed, one after another, holding each other tight to give something to the medics to hold onto as they rush her back inside. And we are proud of ourselves, we are smiling now, our faces wet and our hair in great peaks, and we are moving backward now, one person at a time, retreating back into the lobby of our hospital, and we are its heartbeat, its savior soul.

The Eye

We are all suddenly surprised with the silence—the still and the sun, it comes quickly, so quickly, and most of us know what this means, most of us know to stay put. And so I go to the kitchen and put the kettle on to boil, and while it is heating, I walk into my small bedroom and change from my cleaning clothes into my practice kimono, then back to the kitchen to get the hot water and into the *chashitsu*. Open the door, shut the door. Silence. Everything is as I left it yesterday, all I need to do is pour the hot water into the black kettle and clear my mind, clear everyone away for just this moment.

A hum, really, that is all I need. But a gentle hum at the back of my mind and I can create the proper emptiness. Hear it? The animals hear it; they have quieted in their cages. Everyone hears it. Alec in the lobby of his inn, tense and focused. Kanae on her bicycle, no longer heaving, now able to breathe. Listen to it. It ripples behind our ears while I cross the *tatami* floor, rumbles softly in our minds while I kneel before the kettle and pour the hot water. It vibrates about us while I sit, quiet myself now. With this hum I leave everyone else's story to its peaceful pause. The storm has surrounded us; here, at its quiet center, we are at a stop.

My back is straight, my knees folded beneath me so that my body becomes its own special character, a *moji* that is an alphabet letter of myself, the me who is here only to prepare this tea, the me that means peace. Hear the whisper of the same hum. It is still here, it breathes around us. Watch me take the ladle and admire it, the length of the bamboo handle, its angle in my hands. There, now admired, it is placed gently on the kettle for when I will need it later. Again, I straighten. Listen to the quiet. Now I move the bowls—still we are humming, silently, a vibration in the air between us—I place the bowls before the kettle, lingering with my fingertips on the grain of the pottery, on the tiny raised ridges of the blue glaze. Fingers still full of this touch, I reach for the red scarf tucked into the pocket made between my *obi* and my kimono and I unfold it, run the tips of my fingers along the silk. Pull it taut, fold it. Now it is ready, now I am ready. Again, we must not forget to breathe. I clean the *natsume*, I clean the tea spoon. Gently now. Oh so gently. And the instruments begin to hum with us. The woven floor and my knees against the weave, my straight back and the parallel scroll hanging against the wall, the fragile bamboo and the steam of the water in the kettle. Everything hums.

Take your eyes off of me and look at Alec standing in the lobby of the inn. I am pouring the hot water and he is not in pain, just for this moment, just now while we are paused. And Kanae on her bicycle has started listening to the gentler wind in the trees, to the drops of water falling from the leaves, this typhoon music and her mind is empty and her heart is quiet. And my mind is closed. I pour the water. I rinse the bowl. I am making us all clean again. Hear the flow of water from the ladle into this bowl, see the steam rise up and vanish into the air of this room. Now the bowl is clean, now the spoon is clean. Prepare the whisk. Everything in its place.

Now I measure the tea. The fragrance of the powder reaches me, reaches all of us. We breathe in together. Here, right here, we are all in the same story. I am not telling this story; it is happening to us. I click the slender bamboo spoon against the side of the bowl and the powder falls into the scooped base. Tap. Just once. It is done. As he stands, hands folded and waiting, Alec hears the click, prepares himself for what will come. The green of the tea in the base of this black bowl is a color harmony whose richness empties us completely. Here, we are all at peace. This pause does not ask us to be happy, does not remind us that we are sad. It is nothing. We find ourselves in the space between the rich green and the shiny black. There. Only there.

Do not replace the tea spoon too sharply on the *natsume*. It does not deserve to be dropped now that its purpose is concluded. We honor it for its contribution. We place it upward, tilted. We are grateful. Now to the ladle again, an extension of our own arm, a way to bridge the impossible distance between our sensitive skin and the heat of the boiling water. The steam rises from our ladle, trails through the air. We pour the water into the tea bowl, against the tea powder, letting it race and press against the porcelain. Here is the only violence of this ceremony. The heat of this water is the strongest force we allow into this room. It is a necessary violence.

Take the whisk, this gentle curving tool and stir the tea, around with the wrist, scratching against the bowl. Faster now, careful not to spill. The hum grows louder, we are reaching the end point of our pause. We are climbing toward this ending with gentle hands and a quiet mind. Stir. Breathe. Stir. Whisk it quickly. Smell the damp leaf smell of the absorbing tea, the hint of hot porcelain beneath these fingers. Slowly my back has folded forward, my neck tipped down to watch my task. As the ceremony comes to its finish, the shape of the *moji* made by my body has softened, relaxed. I replace the whisk on the floor and lift the tea bowl. Such a heavy object, filled with such promise. I turn it in my hands, carefully, gently.

And now I give it to you. I give it to Alec. I give it to Kanae. I give it to everyone here in Komachi. I take a sip myself. It is seconds only, warm green seconds when we drink together from this tea bowl and breathe in the silent steam, when we listen to the hum that has lifted us up, that has given us pause. We finish the tea.

霧島

Ken'ichi Chester sits reworking a drawing of an *Apis florea* honey bee, not for an article he will soon publish, not because he needs to finish last-minute work for the weekend, but because it is his favorite, and so he glides the pencil over the sheet of paper in soft, careful strokes, creating the bee's silver-colored beard, he traces out the creature's slender wings and lifts his pencil to make the lines as light, as faint, as possible. Today this little corner of the hospital waiting room has become his own, two chairs, a small low table to rest his bag and notebook, empty paper cups for the tea he sips while he waits and watches and hopes.

"Your work is as passionate as your sister's, I hope you know that," said Alec to Ken'ichi years and years before.

Ken'ichi had bowed, trying not to smile; Megumi was the artist and Ken'ichi the scientist.

Ken'ichi stares at the *A. florea* he has drawn, a male specimen and so much thinner, much more fragile than the female he is meant to serve, and the truth is in the next pencil scratch—this truth: that he might never see his father again—and his pencil stops, midway through the arc of the bee's transparent wing, and Ken'ichi must take a little extra air into his lungs, a breathpause of disbelief. He has never put much faith in the imaginary, why waste his time wondering about intangible, made-up problems or ideas when the real world is fascinating enough, so much complexity in everything around him: the insects he studies with their miniaturized lives, bodies and behaviors, his life with Etsuko and how their partnership works its tiny, gradual alterations on their individual personalities, encounters with strangers on the street, coincidences, events, the weather, the world. No, Ken'ichi has never wanted or needed to look past this concrete universe.

His pencil is beginning a new drawing, one with strong lines and angles, a stick tree of a man with round eyes, but before Ken'ichi can finish his picture, the emergency entrance light is bleating and flashing—oh yes, yet again, he has witnessed it come to life already many times today while waiting here at his post—and the hospital's double doors are sliding open to let in the sound of the storm, much calmer now it seems, Ken'ichi is thinking it must be over soon, but there in the space between the open doors is a man holding a teenage girl in his arms, and she's clearly too heavy for him, he is nearly dropping her and calling out for help.

Staff members step forward and they take the girl and lay her out on the floor of the waiting room, just a few meters from Ken'ichi—the girl's lips are blue, her clothing soaking wet, her arm bent at an unnatural angle, and there is blood, too, something dark on her sleeves, or is it mud? and the man who brought her in is panting now, staring at the hospital staff as they work, kneeling then standing, kneeling then standing, but the staff are taking the girl now, putting her on a waiting gurney and telling the man to go to reception for all the details and it is only when the man turns to do this that Ken'ichi recognizes him.

"Koizumi-san?"
Yes, they went to school together, Ken'ichi is remembering it now, a quick flash of baseball games and science club and jokes passed in class beneath the nose of a strict teacher.

The man turns to him and there is recognition in his eyes, too, then a nod, a touch on the arm from one to the other, a greeting of boys-now-men, and then Koizumi is sitting down in one of these hard plastic chairs, he is rubbing his face, and he is whispering, "When I found her, I thought she was dead . . . but she wasn't, and what if . . . what if she had been dead?"

"They will help her, they will help your daughter."

The man looks up, "She isn't my daughter. I found her. In a side street—between my house and my mother's house. She was slumped against a wall, near the entrance to an alley. I have no idea how long she'd been outside."

"She was alone?"

"Why would a young girl be outside in this storm? Alone? Where was her family? Her friends? How old do you even think she is?"

Koizumi looks at Ken'ichi and between them stretches out the same childhood, the same small town, the neat lines of children walking to school in red caps and blue uniforms, the safety of Komachi's streets, mothers in aprons waving from doorways, fathers at dinner and on Sundays, and they know this wasn't all perfectly true. They remember the boy beaten by his father, they remember a car accident and the rumors of alcohol, but they can't help seeing a shadow line somewhere, a *then* versus a *now*, and they are thinking about what we are all discussing these days: knife attacks at elementary schools, girls who play at being women, drugs to make us all smarter, drugs to make us all forget we will never be smart enough.

"And her arms—did you see her arms? Those cuts. Old ones and new ones. And so young. She's not my daughter, luckily, but I have a daughter," he is looking at Ken'ichi now, his face losing its edges, his lips sticking high against dry teeth. "What if she . . ."

Ken'ichi is thinking of his father now, wondering how people make these decisions, how does one decide to end a life, because it isn't an easy thing, we aren't so fragile as we think, our bodies stronger than we know, and maybe Ishikawa Sensei should not have been so forthright, maybe we aren't meant to know our own timeline like that, maybe this knowledge is too much for us to bear, and Ken'ichi is wondering if he could bear it, himself, and then up kicks a sharp stone of guilt, because he should not be thinking of himself, but of his father.

His old friend Koizumi is holding his head in his hands now, moaning a little, and Ken'ichi stiffens, wishes Etsuko were here, she would know what to do, would know how to smooth the moment with simple phrases and an offering of tea.

"Stay here," he tells his friend, looking around the hospital again, searching for a purpose, then he sees one—there is relief in his lurch forward. "I'll get you something warm to drink, you are all wet."

And crossing the room toward a row of vending machines, Ken'ichi moves far beyond the hospital, he lets his world expand, he sees his father on a bridge, in a car, or at a pharmacy buying medicines, he sees his father with a knife, a gun, but where would he get a gun, so then he sees his father standing at the edge of a steep cliff—and how many different ways are there to end a life? And how would you choose? And this is where he is stopped, this is where he cannot find a way to let each vision complete itself, because he is shocked really, shocked to acknowledge the breadth of it all, shocked to see he has invented such life, such possibility for his father.

霧島

The phone is out, of course, and cell phones are no longer receiving any signal, but still the old woman does not want to let Alec leave her inn. It is much too dangerous, she tells him, and Sensei you are not well, and so Alec pulls himself up to his full height and he looks down on her gray head and the neat bun at the nape of her neck and he becomes, for the first time in many years, an uncompromising foreigner, he will do as he pleases and what it pleases him to do now is find his family, and the woman is staring at him, and she is not bowing, and she is turning from him and he can tell he has frightened her a little, and the power this gives him becomes a hard little pit inside his stomach.

Here is this man before him, too, and Alec is thanking him, waving away his concerns as well, telling our gentle Fumikaze that he is sorry to have caused him so much trouble, and Alec does not see Fumi turn away, does not see this other man's stricken look, and Alec cannot know, cannot even imagine what this man knows, how his body is still wearing the skin imprint of Kanae's own body, her breath, her anger, and her failed escape.

"Be careful . . . and I . . . " The words are trailing away, nothing is suitable, Fumikaze is leaving the foyer now, quickly quickly quickly on his bachelor feet, up away from this dying man, like a thief he is practically running up the stairs.

Alec does not watch him leave, has already forgotten about him, because already he must go, out into the rain, out into the storm—only, the rain has let up, the wind has calmed, and Alec walks a little more quickly because maybe the storm is over, and maybe it will be a simple matter to right all of the wrongs of the last few days; but what a mess, the car is covered in debris, Alec must wipe away the leaves and pine needles and bits of paper with a cloth, and his breathing grows hard, and every few minutes he is checking his cell phone, watching his battery drain away while the little device searches unsuccessfully for a signal, and now into the car, seated behind the wheel and catching his breath. He runs a hand across his abdomen, a soothing pass of palm and fingers that does not soothe, and he can only grit his teeth and try not to cry out when he turns the key in the ignition and absolutely nothing happens.

Just wait, keep calm, relax your arms, the storm is passing, you have gone too quickly, give your old car a moment and think of where you will go—home, of course, there is no shame in returning home, admitting your flight from the hospital nothing but an old man's pride, a way to avoid what is about to happen to your body, and what were you trying to prove anyway, leaving the care of trained professionals, hiding out in this lonesome valley in this tattered inn . . . oh, but, Alec, and this is the part that hurts, this is the part that is nearly too hard to bear, because yes, and you know this, everyone will forgive you, but not because you're a foreigner this time, not because we expect you to do things differently, but because no one believes you have very much time.

Out of the car and opening the hood, here is a task that will make Alec feel useful, and he pushes at some of the cables, fiddles with their connections, and he peers into the confusion of metal parts and rubber parts and tubes and wires and nothing seems amiss, and the air has grown still and is warming, warming quickly, heat is rising up off the pavement again, rising up around his trouser legs and there is even a little sliver of blue sky streaking across the sky, so back into the car now and hands hovering over the steering wheel for just another minute, thinking. *Where could she be? Where could she be?*

Home, he is thinking, but why would she be there now when she hadn't come for days, and although he knows it would be the sensible thing to do, Alec does not want to drive himself into town and find the hospital or the police station, because there is guilt in this, there is the childish shuffle forward and avowal of wrongdoing, no, no, he wants to find his wife, he wants to sit with her and with this everywhere, just the three of them, a couple and an uninvited guest that cannot simply be asked to leave.

Engage the clutch and turn the key again, now the car is chugging to life, and Alec is breathing quickly through his nose, little breaths of triumph and relief, and that sliver of sky has widened, is becoming a trough, and Alec flicks his gaze from sky to road, from road to sky. It seems the storm has finished, and so what matters is driving carefully, watching for debris, avoiding any flooding—it would not do to prove the town correct by accident.

霧島

Don't move, Jun is thinking, *don't move, don't move, don't move*, and his fat sticky finger is rubbing at his nose to keep the dust from tickling, and he worries he is going to sneeze, and his whole body tenses with this fear but he keeps rubbing and the sneeze stops threatening, he can relax his little head, lets his lips fall against his hands which are now flat on the hardwood floor, feeling the dust beneath Mrs. Kenta's sofa where he has been hiding for some minutes now—he could reach his hand out and touch Mrs. Kenta's ankle, and wouldn't she be surprised, wouldn't she jump and squeal, but he doesn't move his hand because this isn't fair, because she will find him eventually and she will fuss and laugh and slip him another chocolate and tell him he is the best at hide-and-seek, better than any of the other children she minds during the week, and Jun will laugh and agree, because no one is better at finding the perfect hiding space than he is, even Jī-chan says so. Jī-chan says, "Jun, little man! Jun is the winner!" And Jun puffs and smiles because Jī-chan says this in English, Jī-chan always speaks English to him, and his mother has been teaching him, too, and he knows the words, even if he forgets sometimes, and Jī-chan loves to play hide-and-seek, letting Jun hide just about anywhere and then pulling him out from beneath a pile of sweaters in Bā-chan's closet, and reminding him they must put it all back the way they found it, and Jun doesn't mind, he likes helping Jī-chan, he likes laying the sweaters out flat on the floor and folding each arm across the chest, like a soldier being put into a coffin in the picture Mr. Kenta showed him once, and then Jun pats the sweater, making it smooth and flat, then folded once more into a little square flag, so straight and soft, and together they stack the sweaters again.

"If Jī-chan gets medicine he won't be sick," he told his mother, "but maybe they don't have any, or maybe it won't work, so then he will go to the doctor and we'll say good-bye, we'll give him two kisses, just like we did with the cat."

But his mother just said that Jī-chan wasn't the same as *neko-chan* and Jun laughed because it was so funny to think of Jī-chan dressed as a cat. Jun will meow at him tomorrow, he's decided, he will meow and rub his ears and here under the sofa with his twitchy nose and his fingertips soft with the dust, Jun starts practicing his best meow, at first just a little and then loud once he's sure of the sound and then Mrs. Kenta's ankles are turning and she is laughing her loud laugh, swiping her hand down the back of the sofa and tickling the nape of his neck.

"Caught you, my handsome boy, now come out and let's do a puzzle, my legs are too tired for more hide-and-seek."

At the table now with Mr. and Mrs. Kenta and they have given him more puzzles than he can do in an hour, and most of them are too difficult for a child of three, but Jun will never admit this, he will only squint up his eyes and make a joke, or ask for a piece of paper and pretend to write a letter, but for now there are these puzzle pieces and Jun is happy to move them around, lining up the edge pieces and sorting them by color.

"We'll get very little of it up here, now it's for sure."
"This is bad rain, we still have to be careful."
Mr. Kenta drops his hand. "If we didn't know this was a typhoon, we'd call it a summer shower."
"You saw the news, there's bad flooding..."
"There's always bad flooding, and Komachi is..."

Here Jun is paying attention again, and his face scrunches at knowing something and so he says it, he says, "Komachi is a tiny useless town."

Silence rolls over the table, and Mr. Kenta raises his eyebrows and Mrs. Kenta's face flattens out, so now Jun is excited, he pushes five red puzzle pieces into his fist and gets ready to repeat what he's just said, only Mr. Kenta is standing now, looking around for his newspaper Jun thinks, or his math puzzles, the small ones he likes to do in the afternoons and sometimes even lets Jun help, even if Jun can only make hash marks and pretend with his numbers.

"She's an empty person. That's all I can say about it."

But Mrs. Kenta is saying *shhh*, that's enough, and smiling at Jun, and Jun wants to smile but his hands have started to twist, and now he's pushing those pieces right off the table and then taking some more, a whole handful this time, and he's flinging them in Mrs. Kenta's face, and her eyebrows are coming together and her mouth has opened and one of those little puzzle pieces has landed right inside and now Jun is frozen because he'd never thought it possible, to aim quite so perfectly, and the puzzle piece vanishes as she closes her mouth, then she spits it out onto the table and there is nothing to do but laugh, because Mrs. Kenta cannot believe for a second that Jun understood what her husband was saying about his mother, and so she chooses to think he's just played a joke on her, and of course he's a little rascal, so clever for his age and we all know that clever comes with mischievous and so she is telling him to help her pick up the mess, and our Jun is a sweet child and he's already under the table and hunting out those little red pieces and gathering them into his closed fist, and the edge of each piece presses into the flesh of his hand, and there's something about this edge that appeals to him, so he's picking up faster and tightening his fingers even harder.

霧島

It is so quiet now, and I am sitting here with my tea bowl, still holding the warm ceramic although the *matcha* is long gone down my throat and has warmed me, has warmed us all, and we need this warmth because the eye is passing over, passing quickly now, in just a few moments the wind will begin again, slowly at first but slowly only for a moment; the second eyewall is vertical and dense and it is racing up the Oyodo River, working its way up from the coast and toward our little mountain town, and while we still have time, while we have this pause, this breath, while Kanae's bicycle is moving more quickly along the footpaths and through our streets, while Alec's car is moving, slowly still, but moving down the road from the inn, I will tell you of another typhoon that came many years ago.

The first word of any story is always the most difficult—how to hold the pen, how to form the characters, how to get it right. Grandfather told me to sit up straight, that the words would come from my belly, and that hunching over would only make it more difficult for them to move out and so I straighten now, still in the tea room but with my papers and my pen and ready to trace the first dark line of this first word.

風. *kaze*. wind.

See that roof, that gentle two-stroke roof that frames this word, and that roof is the most important part of any wind storm—you see, because without a roof, none of us would have anything to lose.

So I begin with wind, and with a roof, and there is a young girl in her bed, listening, she is always listening—down into another room of the house, where the wind can only beat against the windows, and there sits her father between his two parents, and the words between them are as loud and ripping as the claws of the wind at the roof above her head, and there is another sound stronger than all of us, it is the black sound of a missing body, a perforation in the vibrations of the household, a blank space where there should be a mother.

Now a drop of rain has fallen onto the girl's face, fallen from the ceiling while the first shingles are ripped from the roof—they will slowly peel away throughout this night, pulled away like teeth from a rotten mouth, until the roof beams are bare, until the soft inner parts of this house are exposed to the storm—but our girl doesn't move an inch, she doesn't try to avert her face from the drops of the water because this water is coming from the sky that stretches over the entire town and somewhere out there, beneath that same sky, the water is maybe falling on her mother's head, because this is what they're saying downstairs, they're saying that she has gone, that she has vanished off into the storm, and her father is weeping, unable to make real words this night, and turning already to the bottle of spirits that will eventually silence him completely.

She is only little but she knows already that without her father's words, this night will be written by her grandparents, and she can hear them downstairs, and they are more angry than this storm, they are fighting it out, hurling words across the room, each one already decided upon what has happened and here is Grandmother so sure now, no longer only suspicious thus no longer careful, no longer content with only hints she is speaking of an enchantment and rubbing her poor son's head, she is telling him he could never have known, she is reminding him that this is the risk of meeting a woman from another village, because you can never be sure, it isn't his fault that he didn't see her for what she really was, and that we must be grateful to have discovered the trick so early on, that this vanished being is not worth her son's tears. And Grandfather is howling now, cutting her off with the slam of his fist on the table, telling her to give up this ignorant superstition, you are taking this too far, he is yelling, shut your mouth, he is yelling, remember the child, he is yelling.

"Oh, there is nothing to be done about her, anyway. We will keep her, we cannot help it, oh, this poor half-creature, this black magic soul."

And then her father's roar and the crash of the table, the breaking of the glass, and now our girl is up out of her bed, she is sliding the door open, she is creeping down the stairs, her face wet from the rain and from her own crying, and there is silence below her and the shingles are still popping off the roof and the trees are banging against the windows, and this is when she hears it, her first animal, the only fox that has ever called to her, she hears the hoarse yelp and cry above the howl of the storm, and she has no idea what it is, she knows only that she cannot ignore it, so she is sneaking down through the house, past the closed kitchen door and out into the garden. There it goes again and she stands in the rain, already missing her mother, this half of her now gone, and the injured animal cries again and the girl follows the sound, eyes closed and head down, arms in front of her face for protection, here is another scream, and then she sees it, the fox kit trapped beneath the fallen tree, all mixed up in the mud and the roots, its leg stuck in the earth gap made when the tree fell, and this girl is so quick and her body so small, she can fit herself between these roots and her arms wind easily to untangle this little creature, her hands passing over its fur as she works, and she has got it out in a matter of seconds and it is racing, limping just a little, shaking its leg out, but no longer crying. She has calmed it and given it freedom.

And that last word is all that matters, and I trace it out for the first time in real ink, not water, and now everyone will know this story, and wouldn't Grandfather be proud—but this is all just practice because my story has been long finished, there is another story that needs me now and another storm, and we are getting there, we are almost ready.

霧島

Kanae is riding in circles now, taking one street north, then two streets east and one street south, then one street west and two streets north, and so on and so forth, moving northward and eastward through town, methodically, not even sure what she's doing anymore except moving, pushing her body forward and holding her eyes open, searching and thinking, wondering, worrying, almost in a trance now because Alec isn't going to be standing out on one of these streets just waiting for her to ride up beside him, or is he? Maybe he is, she thinks, maybe he's walking around just like her because she cannot imagine he'd settle for sitting out this problem, she cannot imagine he could sit still with this death-thing they must consider now, surely he must be moving, circling her as she is circling him, turning slowly and tightening their circle, to contain what must be contained, to squeeze it tighter and tighter until they can stand together and maybe there will be no more room for anything else.

The trance is broken suddenly and she almost steers her bicycle down the path toward the cemetery; at the last moment she stops because the police car is too close to be ignored, a sleek black and white shape at the curb, its alarm lights turning but silent, and the gray-haired police officer waves her over and she doesn't run away, she brakes at the bumper, politely descends from her seat, ready to answer his questions: What is she doing out on her bicycle? Does she need a ride? Where is her family? She is nodding and polite, and the more he speaks, the more she is filled with a nervous energy, because he has not recognized her, has not connected her to the story of the missing English teacher, she is simply an older woman

144

out on her bicycle, someone who has made a bad decision and must be scolded into returning home.

"Miyakonojō is reporting major wind damage as the second eye-wall hits, it's coming now, you must return home."

She stares at him a little too long—how curious that his warning to her sounded so feeble, not even the slightest inflection, not the least tremble of concern, he could have been telling her anything, that he just bought a pair of new socks, but she is nodding as she should, she is bowing to him and apologizing for not being more careful.

"This isn't the time to be at the cemetery, you know, look at those telephone lines, look how they're swaying already..."
Still she nods, still she doesn't speak.
"They say it's bad, I just had a call on the radio, they say it's really bad in Miyakonojō, and we're in for it, I think—the gods aren't happy."

Again Kanae must wonder at this man's face, at his complete composure and the bored tone of his voice, so at odds with his words, and he's already looking away from her, looking up into the sky, frowning now. Is he confused? Is he angry? But then he shakes himself a bit and asks her again where she lives and can he take her there.

"No thank you, I'm just down the street, I'll go straight home."
"Yes, go straight away now, there isn't much time," he is saying, looking at the path to the cemetery again. "Don't worry about your ancestors, they'll be all right, they're under the ground, they're safer than the rest of us. If we could get the whole town up to the temple, we'd have nothing to worry about—the highest ground, and those walls won't move an inch in this weather."
But the temple is too small, she wants to tell him, what a ridiculous thing to say, and all those open spaces, surely the *torii* gate would fall on them, surely the trees would be a great risk.

"We're going to need protection," he is saying now, speaking more to himself, mumbling and fervent, and Kanae, despite herself, is curious about this man—oh, I could tell her things about him, but not today—and watching his impassable face. "We should be praying, you were right to come out, really, it's good of you, not many people would do it, but it's not safe yet, we're still in it, you see, so best be getting home, say your prayers at home until we can all go back to the temple and thank the gods for sparing us."

Kanae is bowing to him now, one last time, disturbed a little at his piety because she is not a religious woman, has never been a religious woman, and it is strange to be taken for one, and the thought strikes her that maybe she should have been more careful with theology, maybe she should not have been so quick to dismiss it all; it's too late, she is telling herself, pedaling away now, watching the limp tips of the sodden leaves flutter in the mud along the sidewalk and the edge of the street. And then she is stopping hard, braking fast, she is almost falling from her bike—she remembers, she remembers that once in her life she touched religion strongly enough to have it touch her back, and it wasn't a religion of someone else's choosing but a private moment when she felt she had earned a blessing, and Alec was there, and now she knows there is one place she has not checked, there is one place where Alec might have gone to find her, and so she is back on her bicycle and pedaling again, pedaling hard, and *Alec*, she is thinking so hard it becomes an actual sentence, a plea. *Alec, wait for me.*

霧島

It is really no surprise at all that the Chester house has come to ill-fortune—this he dares to think, this neighbor, Mr. Isamu Nishi, as he steps out into the fetid air, holding his nose, surveying the damage in his garden and checking the sky. It appears to be over, he is thinking,

146

and what a mess, and he'll have to spend the rest of the week righting his flowerbeds and clearing away the debris, and it looks like the creek has risen just enough to threaten his basement, so he'll have to deal with that, too, because that nasty water will ruin his preserves, but first he must . . . yes, it really is his job, such a burden really, but he must go next door and make sure his neighbors are all right.

He is already speaking when one of the daughters—it is Megumi first, and Naomi comes up behind her sister—opens the door, already asking his questions and looking around the doorframe, he is asking about their father and checking their faces, and he is thinking that this young woman is quite impertinent, she is rude to him, she has hardly greeted him.

"But you must be very upset . . . I'm awfully sorry to trouble you . . . I just want to see if everything is all right . . . the storm has really caused a lot of mess . . . is your power still out . . . and have you had any news . . . your father . . . may I speak with your mother?"

Oh, these young girls faces are difficult, and Mr. Nishi isn't sure at all how to speak to them, he chooses to look at the second one, the young woman hiding in the shadows behind this other one, the insolent one, yes, the second woman's eyes are much kinder, even if she is hiding most of her face behind hands that have gone up over her mouth and nose. And they are thanking him, yes, they are saying the words and telling him not to worry, but they do not mean it, he can tell, and this only makes his teeth hurt a little where he clamps them against each other, biting down on what he would like to say.

"Now, now, I'm sure the police will find him . . . and your mother, she is probably resting . . . well, as long as you have no trouble, as long as you don't need anything . . . I say, this storm was a bad one, wasn't it? We won't know until the television comes back on, but then it's always the same thing, isn't it? All those horrid landslide photos and the rivers, I wonder where it might have flooded in Komachi . . . "

And he is already turning away from the girls, already picturing the high waters and broken bridges, the threatened houses, and already he is feeling rather smug for how well he has prepared, his house is never affected and even if the shops in town cannot get fresh food for a week, even two weeks, he has plenty to eat and even enough to share, if someone asks. There, behind him the click of the door, and he is checking the front of the Chester house, shaking his head now, stepping backward and listing the likely places where the earth will give away because of all the rain.

Mr. Nishi has always paid attention to the news, and Mr. Nishi has memorized the names of the little towns and the small villages that are most likely concerned when it comes to typhoon damage—these places are ticked off a list in his head now, even spoken aloud, one small village after another... such unlucky places, and so Mr. Nishi could hardly have expected to see a gulley in his own garden, there, just beside the persimmon tree and right where he usually plants his hyacinth, right at the top of the gentle slope of this small hill where he and the Chesters and a few other families have their homes, and he walks over to inspect it, thinking suddenly of Alec Chester and wondering where his neighbor took himself off to die, and why go out into a storm, why not choose the quiet of your own home, the warmth of your bed, if you must go, and Mr. Nishi is still looking at this gulley when it begins to widen, when it ceases to be a gulley and becomes a deep black crevasse, small fibrous plant roots suddenly exposed as the earth cracks and breaks, and then his eyes are widening and he is yelling out, because the grass beneath his feet is moving too and he must take a few steps backward.

Yes, the earth is slipping Mr. Nishi, please watch your step, and look up now, yes, now, because it is upon us again, the second eye-wall with its vertical winds and heavy rain, and he is looking, good man, he is not oblivious, he sees that the storm was not at all finished, he sees that part of his land is sliding off down the hill and he must move quickly backward, all the way to his steps, and hold on tight, because none of us are expecting the strength of this last push of wind.

Landfall

He remembers the box of painkillers at a bend in the road and taps the brakes without thinking, skidding now, the rear of the car fishtailing on the wet leaves and the mud and the flat thin sheet of water rushing along the tarmac, but the car rights itself and Alec stops nearly in the middle of the road, there are no other cars, and he reaches into the glove box, and there is no telling how long this box has been in here, there are only four tablets anyway, and he swallows all four of them, choking a little, the tiny hard bumps sticking in his throat until he swallows for a second time, a third time.

And then again with his foot on the accelerator, pushing forward, pressing down against the remaining amount of time he has been given, and this is a curious idea because although Shingo was helpful with details on the progression of his pain and the options to keep him numb from it, his friend refused to talk time with him, he said it was simply impossible to know and this—Alec clenches the steering wheel now—is extraordinary, perplexing, and he forces himself to think about it, he says to himself in the car, "I will die in three days," or, "I will die in four weeks," and he tests out any number of combinations but none of it helps, none of it makes any sense, because the pressure of his body against the driver's seat, and the tautness of his skin over his knuckles and the dry sting of his eyes despite all this rain and this wet—all of this is too solid, and he cannot imagine himself away.

He is not afraid of death, he thinks, and here his chin even bobs in defiance, but he is afraid of dying, yes, he admits this, afraid of the pain, of the smell, of knowing his body will betray him, and of no longer having a choice whether to be fastidious or messy. Our Alec has always been careful with his body, has known how shocking it might seem to others, especially here in our little town where everything about his physical person is oversized, and we are sorry but there is no arguing, his death will take this carefulness away from him.

The blast of wind against the door takes him by surprise and the little car is pushed across the oncoming lane and nearly into the rocks over to the right, he twists the steering wheel as the rain hits and he feels his tires slip, the lurch of the car until the rubber finds a new grip on the road; he flicks on the windshield wipers but they cannot do much, the water is too thick and overhead a tree top bends, snaps, but his car is still moving fast enough and he catches sight of the limb falling down into the road behind him—no going back, only forward, but he slows down now, watching about and fighting to hold the car steady, and for the first time now Alec is afraid.

Go slowly, she is telling him, *keep your eyes open.*
Yes, he agrees, hearing her, *just keep moving.*

Something—a rock, a bit of wood, a piece of plastic, it doesn't matter—smacks against the windshield, cracking the glass, not on the driver's side but the crack spiders toward him and then there are little drops of water leaking down onto the dashboard. Alec tenses for the burst of this pane of glass, the rumble of these small pieces about him, but the glass remains intact, and he keeps going, slowly, tires rolling along, bumping over the debris, and the water spilling down the hillside to his right is thick and muddy and he is waiting for the road to give out beneath him, speeding up just a little because he is only a few kilometers from the edge of town, only a short distance from sturdier concrete and fewer hillsides, but then he must stop, because there is a sound like a chorus of humans shrieking and he is looking around for injured people, looking and searching the thinning forest to his left, and then he sees that it is only the sound of the trees bending, bending too far, their protest a high-pitched groan.

He is blocked—a wash of tree debris and rocks and mud has covered the road, Alec is striking the steering wheel now, this cannot be happening, this is not how this day will end, and he is getting out of the car, squinting against the water in his face, feeling stronger now, the edge of his everywhere made blurry with those painkillers, and he surveys the road, there is no way to get the car past, but damn it all, he isn't so far, he's actually close now to the small neighborhood where Kanae grew up—isn't he, yes, he remembers now, all he has to do is walk down the hill a ways and there is a side road that will take him to our street, and so he is tucking his head and shaking the water from his eyes and he is walking, footstep and then another footstep, and he can nearly go quickly now and the road is clear and he is watching the trees, listening for the horrid crack and scream, but nothing else falls, and he must steady himself against the guardrail but the wind will not knock him down, he is too tall, he is still too strong.

The side road is calmer, at a different angle to the drive of the wind and Alec picks up his pace a little, trying to remember who still lives along this road, what was the name of the family that bought Kanae's parents old house? And doesn't Kitauchi-san still live next door? And that other family, with the teenage daughters, didn't they speak together last month about the older one enrolling at The Language Lab? Step, Alec, step, step, step, surely someone will help him, surely someone will know just what he needs to do.

He has reached the top of our street, he can see the houses, there aren't so many and we are all boarded up because of the storm, and the water is running down his face and his body is shivering what with his fever and the wind pushing at him, but there, just a few hundred meters away, is Kanae's old house and he is walking toward it, remembering all those times he came here courting, and he remembers Kanae's father and how his lips trembled when he was being severe, and how Alec knew the man was a little afraid of his future son-in-law…but then he sees the bicycle, coming in his direction, and my God what is a person doing out on a bicycle, but it's someone who will help him, and he tries running now, but no, no, oh no, that won't work, dear Alec, each footfall an agony up his back and side.

霧島

The apartment building is swaying in the wind, and Etsuko is not afraid, she even places a hand on the wall, a simple thank you to the architect and contractors whom she is certain have done their job, because this building is meant to sway, meant to give, just enough, to the violence of the storm—*boom*, the windows shake; but she will step away from these sounds because there, just there, a few centimeters in from her hip bone, at the place where the skin has begun to stretch a little tighter than usual, this is where she feels it, this brief rolling pressure, a tiny foot or elbow pressing back against the soft wall of her uterus, even if her doctor has said it is too early, yes, he said, the baby *is* moving, but Etsuko shouldn't be able to feel it, not for almost two more months.

Nevermind the doctor, Etsuko is certain of what she feels, and she's told Ken'ichi about it—she is not afraid to see his mild disbelief, his gentle shrug, he would not contradict her openly, but she knows he does not believe her, he believes the doctor and the scientists and everyone who has documented the timing of these things, everyone who follows their charts and tells her that in a few weeks she will stop feeling so unwell (she has not really felt unwell at all), tells her that in one month her own heart will be working almost 50 percent harder to support this pregnancy (her heart has been working double since she first started wanting this baby), and tells her that in six weeks they will know whether they are having a boy or a girl (Etsuko knows they are having a girl).

Another gust of wind rattles the windows and the room shifts beneath her feet, and she calculates the distance from where she is standing here in Kagoshima to where Ken'ichi will be standing in Komachi, if he's still at the hospital, and she estimates 103 kilometers between them, and the baby flutters against her again, and she places a hand against her skin, and then she is turning on the news and watching reports of the damage done to Kagoshima Harbor, and she is waiting for the newscaster and his team to turn their attention further up the island but she can only get the local news and so there is no word about flooding in the mountains, no word about Ken'ichi's missing father—the windows are shaking again so Etsuko moves into the bathroom, there are no windows in this room and only the gentle swaying of the floor. She sits now on top of the closed toilet seat and breathes in. Her lungs are greedy and the air in this room always feels stale to her, so she is breathing and rejecting it at the same time, and what she would really like to do is go to the kitchen and open the window and breathe in the wind and the rain.

"You should go to your parents' house." Ken'ichi was standing there at the door of their apartment, his overnight bag on his shoulder, his dying father a twitch of the muscle beneath his eye.

"Our apartment is safer."

"Then invite them over."

"They cannot leave Grandfather, you know that."

His frown grew longer, he came back inside then, even if he was supposed to already be in their car, even if it was not exactly safe to be driving north in the storm that was already strong, but Ken'ichi came back inside and sat down to think about what she should do and Etsuko counted up to ten in her head, then to twenty, then to thirty—keep calm, do not shout, she told herself, he is only trying to love you as he knows best.

He nodded then, decided. "Then I'll call Mariko to come sit with you."

Count to five. Speak gently. "She has her own family."

"Well, go to their house."

"I can be here on my own."

"It's a big storm, what if the power goes out?"

Counting again in her head, then, "I have candles and flashlights and food. The power will come back on."

Ken was shaking his head, an arm on her arm, his face quiet in thinking.

"Listen, why don't I go with you to Komachi. I can help your mother."

"She's far too upset, she will upset you. And what if we find... No, I won't have you shaken by this. And it's better if you rest..." A long pause. "Well, there is nothing to do about it. Please do not go anywhere. You must take care of yourself."

And she agreed, and they said a quiet good-bye, and Ken'ichi placed his hand on her stomach but much too high, it was not for the baby, it was a touch for her, and he made her promise one last time she would stay put, and she nodded at him and closed the door quickly, much too quickly, nearly in his face, but her heart was pounding and the thought in her mind that what she really wanted to do was go to the midwife and ask if it was still possible to take this baby from her body. But no, she didn't mean it, not really, she wants this baby, and it is too late for that, too late for the baby and too late for her, she loves this baby, she is insanely in love with the little girl who will be her daughter in a few months, she is already calling her Momoka-chan, the name that came to her one night in the first few days before the storm.

So Momoka it is, and she says the name to herself in between breaths in this bathroom, and she places her hand on her belly in exactly the right place and she holds it there, and she waits for that light pressure again, a body curved into her own, and the floor is still swaying and the storm is still beating against the building, but here she is fine, here *they* are fine, two people in this little room, and Etsuko knows that when this storm is over and Ken'ichi comes home, she must put an end to his silliness, because pregnancy is not a disease, she isn't ill, she isn't about to break so he must stop trying to carry her around in his hands like a fragile vase. And she wonders if this will work, will it be enough, because it isn't just this, there is also the question of there being three now, no longer just Etsuko and Ken'ichi, but a family of three, and maybe someday four, and here she is gripping the edge of the bathtub a little, just resting with her hand on this cool plastic rim, and she is not worried, she reminds herself, every couple must deal with these varying influences, the legacy of their childhoods, the events of their families, and it does not matter that Ken'ichi isn't wholly Japanese, that his parents are different, it has never mattered—she will repeat this a few more times until it feels less forced—and Etsuko touches her belly, she presses back just a little, a promise at the ends of her fingers, she will make sure he understands, she will make him turn from her a little, make him widen the sphere of his love, show him that they are three now, because this is best, of course it's what's best, and he will see. Won't he?

Every story has a seed—a word, an act, an image; Grandfather used to tell me that even a gardener cannot remember exactly where and when a seed is planted, but when the first sprouts break through our dark volcanic earth, that is the time to pay attention…to stand guard and help the plant grow taller, and we are always standing guard, we are always watching for that first shoot of a leaf and wondering what kind of plant might be waiting below the surface, and then only when it comes and it's grown to its full height can I go backward and remember the day I first touched the seed, pushed it deep into the soil.

Those of us in the neighborhood hadn't seen her for years by then, except on national holidays and the rare weekend, but this was not unexpected because Kanae was away at university in Miyazaki in those days, and she was studying hard, her parents were incredibly proud, and careful to show their pride through standard complaints of her distraction—she is so quick to forget her parents, she is a silly young woman and does not know how to cook for herself properly, we're not so sure this university is a good idea—and so we knew she was busy and we knew she was doing well in her studies, and when she came home after graduation, no one wanted to ask about a husband, perhaps she will marry another teacher, we thought, these young women are waiting so long these days, we thought, nodding then, a little worried perhaps, but she was the same young woman who had grown up on our street, her hair a little longer, yes, her smile just a bit older.

That summer is when he first came and Grandmother was the first to stand shocked on the front porch, the first to stare at his far-too-long legs and wonder at the face below his pale hair while he stood at the Endos' front door, and then we saw Kanae open it and pull him inside, her arm on his forearm, such a familiar gesture, and her smile so big it blinded us on our porch, and so we knew then that she would be leaving us soon, and we only wondered if she would send for her parents from America and would the house go up for sale, and would their children know nothing of our Fog Island Mountains.

But we were wrong, and I was the first to know of their plans to get married, I was the first to tell Grandmother that he wasn't even American—He's from Africa! But he's white!—and that they would be staying in Komachi, that he was a teacher and so on and so forth, and Grandmother clenched her fists a little, some of the other neighbors did too, but slowly, over the months that turned into years, we got used to his long shadow and his great brown shoes and his sloped shoulders, and we especially got used to watching him walk her home in the evening, right up our small street, and we would wait in the dark at our windows and we would watch how he kissed her, we would watch how he held on tight to her hand.

And the years passed and his visits changed, no longer a man walking alone up the street, he came in a car with his wife, our Kanae, right beside him, coming on weekends and evenings to see her parents, and he drove carefully, never too fast, and so it wasn't his fault on that one winter evening when it was time to say goodnight to his in-laws, time to lead his pregnant wife back to their car, time to turn from the driveway onto the street, and he couldn't have seen her dashing out from behind the Endos' back garden, there is no way he could have moved his foot to the brake in time, but she is fast, my *kitsune* is ever so fast, and so the car only bumped her rear hip. Still, what a bump, and she was knocked sideways off of her feet and into the trash can at the end of our street, and she lay there for too long, and she was not moving, and anyone else might have left her there, might have been afraid of this wild animal, might not have dared to get out of the car to see if she was breathing, and wasn't it a cold winter night, and wasn't it warm in that car, but our Alec moved quickly, and so did Kanae, and the two of them saw that she was hurt but not killed, they saw that she was not bleeding, and so they waited there—the two of them, kneeling over her, shivering within minutes, not afraid to touch her fur but knowing also to make it quick and give her space—they waited there for those long minutes of waiting, wondering to each other if maybe she had internal damage or maybe she was just stunned, because they hadn't been going that fast, they really hadn't, and then ... wasn't she beautiful, this from Kanae, and Alec agreed, and they watched my *kitsune* for as long as she needed watching, and when she stirred, when she raised her head and came back to herself, both of them froze, awestruck, humbled, at the light in her eyes, at the fireflash of her fur as she leapt to her feet and was gone.

It is funny, this is not a story that either of them have even remembered, and really, it was only a few minutes of their lives, one of many moments of experience that have lined up against each other to become a lifetime of living, and who would have guessed, not our Alec, not our Kanae, that it was this moment that mattered more than the rest, at least to me, to this old woman with her wild animals and her ink pot, with her healing and her poetry, with her voice that will go out to this town.

霧島

She does not see Alec at the end of the street, she sees only the pavement below her rolling front tire, only the edge of the road, this road she has known all of her life, this road settled into the base of a gorge, just at the opening really, a road dotted with only a few houses and which branches off at its end into trails that wind up the hill through the forest, my forest, and as a child Kanae explored its recesses, hunting insects and gathering pock-marked volcanic rocks from the stream, picking flowers that her mother displayed carefully on the family *yakusugi* chest, and Kanae had a hiding place, too, because all children will find one if they are able.

Kanae is pushing now, knees burning, thighs on fire, pushing past the old *onsen* that is sealed up tight for the storm, canvas slings covering the plate glass windows; still, though, steam is rising from somewhere beneath the resort, escaping through vents in the roof, and Kanae pedals on past this building and quickly past her old home with only a glance at its boarded up face, turning now onto the trail between her former house and mine, a trail that is now paved but was not when she was a child, and she knows exactly where she is going as she finally gets off her bicycle, leaning it up against the low guardrail that runs the length of the trail, keeping walkers hemmed in tight against these steep moss-covered walls, and the sheer gorge walls provide her some shelter from the wind and the missiles of debris that threaten.

Alec is shouting now behind her, but she cannot hear him, she can only press forward on foot, ignoring the click in her ankle, the tightness in her chest, and she is worrying that she will miss the old shrine, because how long has it been? Years and children and work and laughter and time and more years since the week she married Alec, since an afternoon spent quietly at her parents' home, since the suggestion of a short walk into the gorge and the promise of breathing tree scents and pressing pine needles with the soles of their feet and time spent alone, and the thrill of sharing a secret with this man chosen for her, chosen by her, sharing with him a secret from her childhood, and she led him up this very trail and to the rock ledge and she showed him the half-buried rope on the ground, she explained about sacred spaces, she walked him along the little row of statues with their worn-off faces and she showed him the shrine itself, she gave him the shrine, a gift of knowing, and he fingered the peeling paint, he traced the indentations of the characters chiseled in the stone, and he asked her to explain its presence, its meaning, and she invented its history and then admitted that she was making it all up.

And she told him that it had been hidden in this forest for so long that she didn't think anyone even remembered about it anymore, even she had forgotten until they'd headed up into the woods for their walk. It was no longer cared for, long-ago left to weather away and disappear.

And Alec had said, "It'll be ours, then. We can take care of it."

And these words remain, ours, and Kanae repeats them as she climbs the trail, she holds the idea up against the rain at her face.

She showed him where she had left her little girl treasures—stones, drawings, pieces of wood worn soft, beaded bracelets, plastic figurines—and she admitted that she had believed the statues to be her gods, and she'd worried whether a person could have her own gods, but Alec had only smiled, had understood both her boldness and her humility, and he'd helped her clean the shrine that day, he'd looked through the little lacquer box she had not remembered hiding inside the shrine, and they had laughed at the faded bits of paper that had been her girlhood wishes, and together they wrote new ones, secret haphazard wedding vows traced out on whatever scraps of paper they happened to have in their pockets.

The path seems longer than she remembers, but at least she isn't facing the wind head on . . . still, every few minutes a gust tears down through the gorge and she must lean low, tuck her head, and the path begins to narrow and in just a few meters it will start to climb this rainy mountain, and she is breathing hard now, flexing her hands now that they are free from their grip on the handlebars, and it is hard to see out from under the hood of her rain jacket, but this is the trail, she is sure, she remembers, and only for this second does she wonder at her certainty that Alec might be in this place, would he have remembered? What is she thinking? This day and this storm and her escape have done strange things to her reasoning, she almost stops and turns around, but she is so close now, and it won't hurt to pause again, to take comfort in this place, to pray.

She spots the path leading into the hidden shrine, it is just ahead, and she is so focused that she doesn't hear the crack above, she doesn't hear the sudden brush of limbs and leaves on other limbs, and then the branch is upon her, landing squarely onto her shoulders, pushing her down onto her knees and then nearly flat, and her legs are slipping, she is slipping, this path so steep, but she gets a hand on the guardrail to her right, she breaks her slide, and this is when she hears the shout—she hears her name now, she hears his voice.

霧島

Naomi is folding laundry in the basement of the Chester home, folding laundry her mother left to dry a few days before, and her hands are shaking, fingertips unsteady, and she tucks them into the folds of fabric, smoothes them along the creases and into the dips of the collars and hollows of the sleeves, and the faster she moves the quieter they become, and when the entire stack of clothing is finished she picks it up, ready to go back upstairs, but the house is still creaking, the sound of the wind against the roof, and the water running past the ground level window above the utility sink is thick and brown and she closes her eyes against this, she whistles to block out the sound of the storm.

She hesitates on the stairs, would like to carry these clothes upstairs and seek out her sister for the company, but Megumi has been leaving her behind all day, each time finding an excuse to do something in another part of the house, and Naomi knows that her sister cannot bear to be in the same room with her today, and while she knows this isn't an active dislike, it isn't that Megumi cannot stand *her*—still she feels her sister's impatience, knows her own weakness causes this, and out of courtesy she will keep away.

The lights flicker again but this time they do not go out, not like earlier this morning when they lost power for a few hours and then mysteriously regained it, but they have continued to flicker and with each dark second, Naomi shudders, what she wouldn't give to be in her apartment in Miyakonojō, with its modern design, its earthquake- and typhoon-proof girders, its reinforced basement and extra storm gutters, a safe structure to keep the world's unexpected interruptions at bay.

Naomi is still holding that stack of laundry and still poised on that bottom step, and the wind is rattling against that low ground-level window, and somewhere above her Megumi is moving around, but otherwise the rest of her family is out in this storm, running around, risking their lives, and she feels a little rise of panic, a sharp edge of fear, because why can't they be more sensible? Even Ken, she thinks, with a pregnant fiancée who is probably terrified at home in Kagoshima and he's here in Komachi, waiting inside the hospital with dozens of other people, and wherever her parents are Naomi does not want to consider anymore, not just her father but now her mother, not sleeping in her bed as she and Megumi had thought, and they have told the police of Kanae's disappearance, and the police were sorry but said there was nothing more to do than what they are already doing for Alec, double-checking the bridges and rivers, having officers visit those places that should be avoided on a day like today.

I could be out there, too, Naomi is thinking, I could be driving back to Miyakonojō, braving this violent weather to get to someone, too . . .

The idea makes her breathe more quickly, tightens her hand on the banister, not the sudden image of her boyfriend James that rises with the thought, but the image of her own little car hurtling through the wind and rain, up along the flooded streets, the possible downed power lines and blocked tunnels—would she hazard this storm for James? Would he hazard it for her?

"Remember, lamb, nothing is stronger than you." This her father once said to her, on a day much like today, only she was little, still a child, terrified and crying beneath her blankets at every loud knock of tree limb against the roof, at the rattling of the shutters, at the great gusts of wind that pushed even their garden pots off the edge of the back deck where they broke against the low garden wall.

"The wind has empty fingers. The rain cannot come into our house."

English was the language of safety, her father's soft voice telling her there was very little to be frightened of, and Megumi on the other side of the room, trying to help in her own way—"Nao-chan, if the thunder scares you, shout back at it, like this!"—and then Megumi would raise her fists above the futon cover and yell at the ceiling, and Ken, still a toddler, would stare at them all, silent, his eyes wide.

James is from America, from Pennsylvania, and he tells her there are no such things as typhoons or earthquakes where he comes from, there are no high mountains on the horizon, no threatening ocean, and twice he has already mentioned marriage, four times he has invited her to go with him on a visit home; just for a week, he tells her, just to see if you like it, he says, but I know you will love it.

And our Naomi knows she will love it, too, but each time he has asked her she tells him no, for now, she always says she will think about it, because Naomi knows she is not like her mother, not like Megumi, no, she is like her father, she knows she will give up her entire life for this man, so she is holding tight, for now, of the only thing she can control—when her new life will begin.

Naomi is walking up the stairs now, gripping the railing with one arm, carrying the basket of laundry with the other, and crying again because she cannot seem to stop crying these days, and she is placing one foot in front of the other, she is ignoring the shift of the house and the clatter of another tree branch against the roof, and she is promising herself that if her father comes home today, if they find him, if her mother is still safe, she will tell her family about James, she will admit that she is leaving Japan once his short contract is finished, and she knows that her mother will not understand, her mother might even be angry, but her father will know, he must know, he will remember what it feels like to want to give yourself up completely, to lose your own culture, your own language, to exchange one self for another, to become the person it finally feels comfortable to become.

霧島

Alec is running now and shouting again, she has turned to him, is waiting for him, but his feet in their flat soles are slipping, and he, too, must grab onto the guardrail to keep from sliding down this hillside, and the mud and the water and this inside pain that is all his own, that is everywhere now, a most unwelcome witness to this moment, but he has climbed the path, with this rain on his face and this wind above and all around them, and this small river that is now overfull, that is climbing its own banks, coming nearer to the path, but he has made it and here they are together, at last, and quickly Alec is brushing the mud and leaves from her shoulder and there are words shouted out at each other, a chaos and tumble of words, none of them mean anything, and Alec's hands are shaking and here is not a place for anything but this first touch of one hand to the other, and they are pulling each other up the path toward the narrow opening in the rock wall, and Alec can feel her finger bones, the solid bump of each of her knuckles against the inside of his larger hand.

They can hear the sound of the earth giving away somewhere up above them, up higher in the forest on a nearby slope, but maybe coming here, and the crash of a tree makes Alec freeze, he is still shaking, this violence around them, but Kanae is pulling him still, and here are these little statues with their rubbed off faces and puddles of water now at their stone feet, and Alec is gripping Kanae's hand too tightly now, a mixture of anger and relief because when he saw her nearly fall, when he saw the branch land on her—and he thought it hit her head, he thought . . . no, it doesn't matter, she is okay, she is the one gripping him, crushing his hand, and her hands are shaking too, but she pulls him under the rock ledge, as far back into the natural cave as they can go, and the rocks are dry here and though the storm-ripped forest sounds like a war, they could almost hear each other if they would dare to speak.

He does not see her as she turns to him, only the outline of her face and the whites of her eyes and teeth, both so sharp in the storm darkness, but he can close his eyes and know her entire face, the tiny mole by her eyebrow and the uneven rise of her two cheekbones, the tight slope of her nose, the small round point of her chin, and this is the face that has been with him for a lifetime, his lifetime, now a finite period, and she is saying something to him now, she is throwing words at him, unblinking, and the look of her anger is as terrifying as the crashing and hurling of the typhoon as it rips up the forest, and then she stops suddenly, she listens, and he is breathing too heavily, all the adrenaline of his flight and his walk from the car now collapsing over him, and he is growing dizzy and her hand moves to his forehead and there is a moment when they cannot look at each other, when their hands, still touching, are empty and enraged.

What matters now is the geography of this little shrine, and what part of the forest it claims sacred, because this storm is always moving, and our Komachi is only a small town—quickly passed over, quickly damaged, quickly released—and although the wind is still driving down upon us, the storm has shifted its center, it has moved to a higher elevation and the peaks of the Fog Island Mountains are offering their resistance, slicing the wind, carving it up into lesser gusts and flipping it back upon the storm itself, and slowly, starting from now, right now, this storm will leave us.

Alec is still catching his breath and Kanae is staring at him, and he knows this frightened face of hers, the one she wore when her children got hurt, when Megumi announced she was pregnant and alone, when her father asked to come live with them after her mother died, and yes, he remembers this same face, too, from their period of courting when it would sneak into their more serious conversations, when it surprised them both in a moment of happiness, and he is nodding at her now, able to look at her again, because forever is such a terrifying thing but they have already managed one forever and they have done just fine with it.

Kanae now reaching around him, fumbling with the crannies of this rock ledge and finding her way to the little square of shrine and there tucked behind the box, still inside the rock wall, after so many years—perhaps someone has been keeping it safe—is Kanae's little lacquer box, the one she showed him so long ago, and she is holding it out to him, and he is taking it, opening it, and there between his fingers are the slips of paper they once tucked inside.

He unfolds the papers to see that the words are gone, vanished completely, nothing left of his and Kanae's forty-year-old hand-writing, and this betrayal is such a shock that he must blink back against it, wipe it away from his face.

But Alec presses the papers into Kanae's hand anyway, and the words they wrote are coming to him, *I promise . . .*

She is holding herself now, she has not reached out to touch him again, and her arms are like a wall to him, wrapped over her chest and her eyes are wide and she is stepping back, moving toward the forest again, escape in her feet once more, but no, Alec stands now, bumping his head on the top of the overhang, the last time he will feel like a giant in our midst, and he is stepping toward her, pushing them both into the storm, into the rain and the wind that have been beating at them for days now. But this time they will stand here together, and watch their hands now, the strength of each hand as it holds the other, and their feet do not move, and although she hesitates the words come back to her as well, the words they first said together so many years before, and they are whispering the words because the sound isn't important anymore, what matters is remembering how they did this once, and they are whispering and trembling as they step back beneath the rock ledge of this forgotten shrine, and they are the words. They are the words and this storm.

霧島

I am not near the shrine this time but I hear them all the same, we all hear them, all of us in Komachi as this storm crawls away from us, and as we are stepping out from our homes and these buildings and into the ragged sunshine and the still-strong wind, but this is no longer a typhoon, this is now the aftermath, the moment of retrieval, of taking stock, of wandering around our homes and looking at the damage. And so here I am checking on the animals, pulling at the ropes I've used to tie the shed and looking at the back window that has broken, just a crack really, but there is water on the floor and my grandfather's cabinet has shifted again because the wood is rotting at the base, one of the sides will collapse soon and I know how I will spend the next few days, working to repair it, drying out the wood with a fan and patching, as I have patched it already so many times before. But the animals are fine, the hares have come out from their burrow-box and are looking at me, their ears up and alert, still wary of the sounds outside, but even they know the worst is over, and then it comes, it hits me hard and I must freeze, rope in hand, here is the yip and yowl and the flutter of wings and the grunting of the badgers, the skitter of the deer, all of them, every animal in my forest, and what could this mean?

I am dropping it all now, I am out of the shed and through the *sugi* and up into the woods and this slippery mud will not stop me, these fallen branches and the still-falling water from the tree tops, and the wind at my back, none of this will stop me because the animals are calling me, and my old heart is pounding now, and I'm wondering if this is my last day, if this is how it will go, that the animals will call me deep into the forest and of course I will go, I am ready to give myself up to them, I am, and so I am still running, still following the howl and grumble, the *shree* of the hawk, and where are they leading me, not toward the shrine, no, away toward the gorge, to the natural sulfur spots and hidden holes, here I must walk carefully, and then I need no longer walk at all, because here she is.

The animals are silent now, vanished away and hidden, and I fall to my knees, and I crawl to her body, to what hasn't been broken, and there beneath my fingers is the whole flat panel of her red fur, this fiery broad side of her, the black socks of her feet, only three of them visible, the other twisted and muddied, and her white beard, and I am rubbing her down and telling her to come back, telling her she must be okay, but her body is still, her body will not move for me, and when I pick her up she is empty in my arms, she is only a memory, a child's toy, a rumor, and I carry her back down through the woods, and we pick our way again through the mud and the branches, across the swollen stream and it takes twice the time to get her home, she is not heavy but I am weighed down, and then, unexpectedly, we are in my backyard and I can lay her out near the shed.

Watch me now, watch me looking up at the sky, because the wind has flattened itself out into a steady push, no longer truly violent, and the rain has stopped falling, and the air is already heating up again, this late summer air will fight against the coming of the autumn with all its might, and my hand is on *kitsune* and I am breathing deeply, and the sky is clearing now, we will all be able to breathe again, and I turn my thoughts to town, to all of us in our houses or looking outside, and there are so many faces at so many windows, and so many people on their porches, they too are looking up at the sky, watching this light change, growing lighter now, for an hour or so as the storm moves off of us, as our island comes back to itself, and then it will grow dark again as the evening steals in, as the news reports are collected and the stories of what happened are broadcast to us all, some correctly, some needing correction, and already for this hour there are things we can repair, we can cover up the broken windows and move furniture from the water, we can collect garbage from the river, and wrap our injured elbows and our twisted ankles, find bandages for the small cuts and salve for the bruises, and husbands will be calling their wives, saying no, do not worry, I'll be home soon, and mothers will be calling out to their children, saying, it's over, it's time to see what must be done, and lovers will be telling their beloveds that yes, I am ready, and slowly, quietly, all will be put right.

So I pick up this thin body again, wrap her up in the sheet I've laid her upon, take her up the steps into the house, the house that maybe, just maybe, she knew from before, and then for this hour until the darkness comes, I will sit with her, and so together we walk into the kitchen, into the house, and Grandmother is here again, and I am nodding to her, and there is Grandfather, too, and he is nodding to me, and I know that it's time, now that the story has finished, and so I lay out my *kitsune*, and I pull out that first sheet of paper, and I am reaching for my pen and thinking hard for that first word, and when it comes to me, it will all come so easily, and there will only be one story to tell, and it is this one, and so I begin...

So this is our town, our little Komachi...

Glossary of Japanese Words

ai: love, a person's sweetheart

aka-chan: baby

Ashi ga ippon shika nai kono kaeru: This frog only has one leg

bā-chan: grandmother

chashitsu: a room or small house meant for performing the Japanese tea ceremony

Gaijin-san: a way of addressing a foreign person in Japan, literally "Mr. or Ms. Foreigner"

genkan: entranceway; front door

irasshaimase: welcome; greeting

Jī-chan: grandfather

juku: a private school

kanji: system of writing

kaze (風): wind

kendōgi: uniform; outfit for performing and practicing Kendō

Kirishima (霧島): The name of a mountain range on the Japanese Island of Kyushu; the characters literally mean "Fog Island"

Kirishima Renzan wa kazan bakari desu: The Kirishima Mountains are nothing but volcanoes.

kitsune: fox; fox spirit

koan: paradox

Komachi (小町): The name of a town; the characters literally mean "small town"; also a synonym for *beautiful* or used as a noun to describe a woman or girl, literally "a beauty"

mado (窓): window

matcha: tea

matte imasu: waiting

mochi: rice cake

moji: written character

neko-chan: cat

obi: sash for a kimono

ohayō gozaimasu: good morning

okāsan: mother

onigiri: hand-rolled rice balls

onsen: hot spring; bathing facility

natsume: tea caddy

ryokan: traditional inn

saru: monkey

senbei: rice cracker

shōchū: distilled beverage

shōshō omachi kudasai: please wait (a moment)

shujin (主人): husband

shūjin (囚人): a prisoner; convict

shūjin (衆人): the public; the people

sō da nē: hmm, yes, it would seem so

sugi: cedar tree

Nani mo tabete nai desu yo ne: you haven't eaten anything, right?

tatami: woven floor mats

tenisō: metastatic lesion

torii: red gate at the entrance to a shrine

yakiniku: grilled meat

yakusugi: 1,000-year-old cedar tree

yukata: robe; informal kimono

Author's Note

Komachi is a fictional town, but it is located somewhere near the very real Kirishima Mountain Range of southern Japan. The grandson of the sun goddess Amaterasu was the mythological ancestor of Japan's first emperor and, according to Japanese legend, he descended to the earth for the very first time within these mountains. The quote from the *Kojiki* that opens the novel is taken from the description of that first descent. It is meant to highlight the privileged place these volcanic mountains occupy within Japan's storytelling tradition.

Komachi (小町) literally means "small town," and while there are a few villages named Komachi in various areas of Japan, there is no Komachi in the Kirishima area. Komachi is more often the name of a neighborhood, a district, or even a restaurant or business. When writing *Fog Island Mountains*, I was wary of using a real place. Mainly because the novel's Komachi has its own internal geography, which—along with its relationship to the larger Kirishima region—is meant to be entirely fictional. But the word *komachi* can be used in a different way. A ninth-century Waka poet named Ono no Komachi was renowned for her great beauty and tragic love affairs, and *komachi* has since become a synonym for "a beauty." As it happens, her story has been written and rewritten and shifted to suit its audiences. This was an influence on my conception of the effects of Azami's own rumor-filled upbringing, as well as what she is doing in telling Alec and Kanae's story.

"Come and Sleep" is the first known Japanese folk tale about a fox-woman bewitching a man and becoming his wife in human form. It is taken from the eighth- or ninth-century *Nihon Ryōiki*. The version I most often consulted comes from *Miraculous Stories from the Japanese Buddhist Tradition: The Nihon Ryouiki of the Monk Kyouka* by Kyoko Motomochi Nakamura (Harvard University Press, 1953).

Also, several other books became a part of my working bibliography for the novel: *KOJIKI: Translated with an Introduction and Notes* by Donald L. Philippi (Princeton University Press and University of

Tokyo Press, 1969); *Japanese Tales* by Royall Tyler (Pantheon, 1987); *Romances of Old Japan* by Madame Yukio Ozaki (Simpkin, Marshall, Hamilton, Kent & Co., 1919); *The Tale of Genji* by Murasaki Shikibu translated by Seidensticker (Knopf, 1976); *Japanese Love Poems: Selections from the Manyōshū* edited by Evan Bates (Dover Publications, 2005); *Seven Japanese Tales* by Junichiro Tanizaki (Knopf, 1963); and *Kitsune: Japan's Fox of Mystery, Romance and Humor* by Kiyosho Nozaki (The Hokuseido Press, 1961).

Acknowledgments

I would like to express my deepest gratitude to the late Christopher Doheny and to his family. And to Beth Anderson at Audible as well as Noreen Tomassi at the Center for Fiction. Also to Dani Shapiro, Meghan O'Rourke, and Ann Hood for selecting *Fog Island Mountains* and giving it this chance for publication. I am extremely grateful to Ron Formica, Laura Colebank, Hilary Eurich, Amy Fernald, John Molish, and everyone else at Tantor for their enthusiasm and support, and especially to Karen Ang for her careful editorial eye and kind comments.

I would also like to extend my love and thanks to Mitchell and Mary Jones for giving me the extraordinary gift of being born in southern Japan. To Claude Bailat and Emiline Jones Bailat, thank you, always, for your love, enthusiasm, and boundless support. To Jennifer Jones Barbour and Josh Barbour, your love and friendship mean the world to me. To Nancy Freund Fraser, your editing skill and your friendship are invaluable gifts. To Steve Himmer, it is my great fortune to count you as a friend and writing colleague—thank you for everything. To Kimberly Bamberg, Rhiannon Kruse, and Liz Robertson for your incomparable friendships. To Rina Kanemaru for your willingness to answer my questions, no matter the time of day. To Matsumi Fukae (and your entire wonderful family) for years of friendship. To Nicola Slack, thank you for being the first to share my writing dream in our tiny studio in Kobayashi so many years ago. To Adam Meinig for not laughing. To Laura McCune Poplin, Sophie Knight, Margaret Saine, Iris Kuerten, Colleen Hamilton, Rosie Roberson, Emily LePlastrier Civita, Laurie Sanchez, and Martha VanKoevering for being my very first readers and all-around bookish friends.. To Tony Bradman for your eternal kindness and encouragement. To Frederick Reiken and DeWitt Henry for your insight and mentoring during my MFA. And finally, to Mr. Ronald Norman for taking me seriously when it mattered the most.

Michelle Bailat-Jones is a writer and translator. Her novel *Fog Island Mountains* won the Christopher Doheny Award from the Center for Fiction in New York City. She translated Charles Ferdinand Ramuz's 1927 Swiss classic *Beauty on Earth* (Onesuch Press, 2013). She is the reviews editor at the webjournal *Necessary Fiction*, and her fiction, poetry, translations, and criticism have appeared in a number of journals, including the *Kenyon Review*, *Hayden's Ferry Review*, the *Quarterly Conversation*, *PANK*, *Spolia Mag*, *Two Serious Ladies*, and the *Atticus Review*. She lives in Switzerland.